TRAILER TROLLOP

THE PROWL • THE BURGLAR WHO COUNTED THE SPOONS • THE BURGLAR IN SHORT ORDER

KELLER'S GREATEST HITS

HIT MAN • HIT LIST • HIT PARADE • HIT & RUN • HIT ME • KELLER'S FEDORA

THE ADVENTURES OF EVAN TANNER

THE THIEF WHO COULDN'T SLEEP • THE CANCELED CZECH • TANNER'S TWELVE SWINGERS • TWO FOR TANNER • TANNER'S TIGER • HERE COMES A HERO • ME TANNER, YOU JANE • TANNER ON ICE

THE AFFAIRS OF CHIP HARRISON

NO SCORE • CHIP HARRISON SCORES AGAIN • MAKE OUT WITH MURDER • THE TOPLESS TULIP CAPER

COLLECTED SHORT STORIES

SOMETIMES THEY BITE • LIKE A LAMB TO SLAUGHTER • SOME DAYS YOU GET THE BEAR • ONE NIGHT STANDS AND LOST WEEKENDS • ENOUGH ROPE • CATCH AND RELEASE • DEFENDER OF THE INNOCENT • RESUME SPEED AND OTHER STORIES

BOOKS FOR WRITERS

WRITING THE NOVEL FROM PLOT TO PRINT TO PIXEL • TELLING LIES FOR FUN & PROFIT • SPIDER, SPIN ME A WEB • WRITE FOR YOUR LIFE • THE LIAR'S BIBLE • THE LIAR'S COMPANION

WRITTEN FOR PERFORMANCE

TILT! (EPISODIC TELEVISION) • HOW FAR? (ONE-ACT PLAY) • MY BLUEBERRY NIGHTS (FILM)

ANTHOLOGIES EDITED

DEATH CRUISE • MASTER'S CHOICE • OPENING SHOTS • MASTER'S CHOICE 2 • SPEAKING OF LUST • OPENING SHOTS 2 • SPEAKING OF GREED • BLOOD ON THEIR HANDS • GANGSTERS, SWINDLERS, KILLERS, & THIEVES • MANHATTAN NOIR • MANHATTAN NOIR 2 • DARK CITY LIGHTS • IN SUNLIGHT OR IN SHADOW • ALIVE IN SHAPE AND COLOR • AT HOME IN THE DARK • FROM SEA TO STORMY SEA • THE DARKLING HALLS OF IVY

The Classic Erotica Series

I Sell Love
Kept
Lust Weekend
Of Shame and Joy
Passion Nightmare
Sin Bum
The Sin-Damned
Sin Hellcat
Sexpot!
Sintime
A Strange Kind of Love
So Willing
Trailer Trollop
Tramp
The Twisted Ones
The Wife-Swappers
A Woman Must Love

TRAILER TROLLOP
Copyright © 1961, by Lawrence Block
Original Publication, writing as Andrew Shaw

All Rights Reserved. This book or parts thereof may not be
reproduced in any form, stored in any retrieval system, or
transmitted in any form by any means—spoken, written,
photocopy, printed, electronic, mechanical, recording, or
otherwise through any means not yet known or in use—
without prior written permission of the publisher, except
for purposes of review.

Cover & Interior by JW Manus

A LAWRENCE BLOCK PRODUCTION

TRAILER TROLLOP

LAWRENCE BLOCK

Chapter 1

JAN PARTRIDGE, THE FORMER Mrs. Jack Appleton, rode a Greyhound bus from Laredo to San Antonio. A puddle-jumping airplane carried her from San Antonio to Houston, where she waited for an hour before carrying her single small suitcase onto a jet liner bound nonstop for New York. She sipped gin-and-tonic on the airplane, left her seat belt fastened for the duration of the flight, and deplaned in a state bordering on intoxication at Idlewild International Airport.

A Carey Transportation Service bus carried her from Idlewild to the West Side Airlines Terminal on 42nd Street for the sum of a dollar and change. Still carrying her suitcase, she left the terminal and crossed the street to the Hotel Commodore. The desk clerk had her reservation. A bellhop took her suitcase, leaving her with only her small black handbag to carry, and led her to her room on the twelfth floor. She looked quickly through her bag for her change-purse, missed it the first time around, and gave up the search, handing the bellhop a dollar.

"Happy Fourth of July," she told him. "Now go away."

He looked at the bill, which was a much larger tip than

the automatic quarter, and started to thank her profusely. Something in Jan's expression told him that she wanted to be alone. He nodded briefly and disappeared.

She stood for a moment and looked at the closed door. She turned and walked to a window, drew the shade and looked out at New York. Her room was frigidly air-conditioned; the city was not. New York baked in the sticky heat of late afternoon in mid-July. Not the Fourth of July at all, she thought. Not by a week or two. There were no firecracker displays over the Hudson, just as there was no brass band on hand to demonstrate over the homecoming of Janice Partridge.

Homecoming.

Home, she thought. Home is New York again. Home is always New York if you start out there. Because the rest of the world puts up its cold iron fence and shuts you out. The friendly little mid-American small towns welcome you like the Bubonic Plague. If you start in New York you belong in New York. And nowhere else.

All the traveling left her feeling as though she had slept in her clothes for forty days and forty nights. And the drinking, which had made the trip go that much faster, had also increased perspiration. She turned away from the window, the shade lowered once more, and began to undress.

A tall, stately girl. Red-brown hair, long, swept back. Deep eyes that were sometimes green and sometimes grey. A full, sensual mouth. A body that might have looked queenly if it were not quite so full-blown, so damnably voluptuous. Big, high-tipped breasts with red rubies at their tips. A slender waist. A stomach slightly rounded. Soft-yet-firm buttocks quite pinchably pink.

Long, perfect legs. Good feet.

She walked into the gleaming bathroom. There was a full-length mirror on the inside of the door and she took a fast look at herself, noting with approval the perfection of her body. A good body, though. A damn good body. A body built for love.

Which, it seemed, was a waste.

A shame.

She turned quickly from the mirror. She adjusted the shower curtain in the tub, turned on the water and managed to reach the proper balance of hot and cold. She took a cake of fresh soap from the sink and unwrapped it, dropping the wrapper into a wastebasket. She stood still for a moment, thinking of MacNamara Army Base, thinking of the tiny town of Coldwater just fourteen miles from the base, thinking of a man named Jack and a wild-eyed girl named, annoyingly, Lily Sue. She closed her eyes.

She opened them, then, and looked down, and saw that her hands were knotted into hard fists with her fingernails biting into the palms of her hands. The muscles in her legs were tight as steel bands. She managed to laugh at herself without amusement. Then she opened her fists, relaxed, and stepped into the tub and under the shower.

The shower was a mindless act—warm water flowing over breasts and belly and thighs, soap worked into pink flesh, skin turning clean and fresh again under the treatment of soap and water. She showered and soaped and rinsed, and when she was done she stood for a long moment with her arms at her sides and the hot spray of water centered upon the back of her neck. She did not think about anything at all. The hot water sapped her strength and drained the nervousness and tiredness and pain from her mind and body. When she left the tub she was refreshed and relaxed, if not happy.

She dried herself off, then returned to the room proper and opened her suitcase. There were clean clothes in the case which would tide her over until she had a chance to do some shopping. She took the clothes from the case and laid them out on the bed. Then she found something else in the suitcase. So she did not get dressed then. Instead she sat down quite naked on the edge of the bed, her long legs crossed at the knee, her breasts bare and vibrant, her skin glowing from the soap-and-water treatment.

She sat on the edge of the bed, naked as a featherless jaybird, and read her divorce decree.

THE TOWN OF COLDWATER was no place for a couple to learn to be married. It was a vile enough place to be even if, God forbid, one happened to have been born there. When you were an out-of-town couple, an enlisted living off-post with his wife in a nauseous little trailer camp as hopelessly ingrown as the town of Coldwater itself, things became just that much worse. When you and your husband weren't matched too marvelously to begin with, and when you were a New York girl with a hick hubby living among men and women from every one-horse town in the nation, things quite quickly shifted to impossible.

And impossible was the word for it.

They shouldn't have married in the first place, when you came right down to it. Jack Appleton had been an Arkansas college student who had somehow wound up at NYU on a scholarship, one awarded mainly in consideration of his prowess with a basketball. Jan Partridge had similarly been at NYU, not on a scholarship but on the joint insurance policy her parents had left behind them when they picked the wrong airplane back from a weekend in Chicago. They had met, with Jack a senior and Jan a junior, and they had wound up in bed and that was that.

That had most definitely been that, she thought. Neither she nor Jack had gotten into that bed a virgin. Her experience had been limited to a few of the boys she had dated, and his had been limited to the girls who had gotten within ten feet of him. But who had wanted to go to bed with a virgin? Not she, and not he. What they had found in that bed—the bed in Jan's small apartment on Christopher Street, had been magnificent.

They were good in bed, pure and simple. Jack's hands

on her breasts had felt like no other hands ever before. Jack's mouth on hers, Jack's body pressing down on her own good body, Jack's hands squeezing her, and Jack's body filling her with the full force of his love, driving her to the peak of passion, a peak she had never so certainly reached before. It was good for her, almost too good, and when it was over that first time she thought it had been a dream, that in reality it had not happened at all.

But it had happened, all right.

More than once.

Quite frequently, as a matter of fact.

Better every time.

And then, near the peak of an earth-shattering, bedspring-busting love affair, graduation came. Jack Appleton received, in all too rapid succession, a diploma certifying him to be a Bachelor of Arts, a letter beginning *Greetings* and requesting him to report for induction into the armed services, and a license which, when duly signed by the proper vested authorities, united him and one Janice Partridge in bonds of holy matrimony.

There was barely time for a honeymoon. They flew to Miami Beach for a weekend and left without a suntan for the simple reason that they never left the hotel room. Then basic training—a rat-trap town in Georgia, a single room in a flypaper rooming house where she lived alone and waited for him. They never had the chance to be married in that town. She saw him for odd short intervals. She would be waiting in the room, and he would rush in, and their clothes would disappear and they would be on the bed and the old biddies downstairs would listen to the bedsprings and have something to snicker about.

That was basic training. Eight miserable weeks of it, eight weeks at the conclusion of which Jan Partridge Appleton had her husband back.

More or less.

For better or for worse.

He had a brief furlough at the start and they spent it introducing Jan to his parents. That was the only time Jan had the displeasure of meeting Mr. and Mrs. Appleton, and for that she was heartily thankful. They were sort of a Tennessee Williams version of Ma and Pa Kettle. Mrs. Appleton sat on the front porch sucking on a corncob pipe like Mammy Yokum, to further confuse the imagery. And Mr. Appleton drank bootleg liquor day and night and stared at Jan as if she weren't wearing any clothes. She was positive the old bastard was crouching outside their door every night when they made love. And she couldn't stand the way he took hold of her hand, or gave her a most unfatherly kiss. A man who wanted to seduce his daughter-in-law was bad enough on the Broadway stage, but in real life it rapidly became unbearable.

Then, happily, they left Arkansas. Jack scraped up the money to buy a second-hand Chevy, and they somehow scraped up a little more money and bought a third-hand

Rio Rancho Mobile Home. That, Jan discovered, was an annoying Madison Avenue colloquialism for *trailer*. It was a tiny piece of excess baggage that was clumsily attached to the tail end of the Chevy. It was barely mobile, and certainly not a home. And it would have taken more than a heap of living to effect such a transformation.

And so they trailed their way to MacNamara Army Base, and thus to the town of Coldwater. Coldwater didn't exactly make Kentucky look like Heaven, since very little could. But Coldwater definitely looked like hell. It took Jan a while before she could decide which she liked less—the town in itself, a collection of skulking Jukes and Kallikaks who couldn't have loathed the soldiers more if they had been Russians, or the trailer camp, row upon row of immobile homes with their fruity attempts at gardens, with their silly lace curtains and their we're-all-soldier-boys-and-their-little-wifies air of provincial in-groupishness. She hated them both.

It wasn't the impossibility of making ends meet on a private's salary, she thought. It wasn't the cramped living conditions or the lack of luxury. She was not a girl who was accustomed to luxury, or who craved it. She would have willingly put up with a two-room cold water railroad flat on Rivington Street—if it had been a house with love in it.

It wasn't that. It was the people, and it was what she and Jack became to each other. But mostly the people, because that started it. Sartre was right. Hell was other people. And there was no exit in sight—

JAN YAWNED. HER FINGERS opened and the divorce decree, printed in Spanish on one side and in English in the other and certifying that she and Jack Appleton were no longer man and wife, fell to the floor. A Mexican divorce—about as difficult to obtain as a pack of cigarettes from a vending machine. But perfectly legal when both parties consented to it. And she had consented readily enough.

And why not? Bradwell Finch had wanted Jack Appleton for a son-in-law. Jack had wanted Lily Sue Finch for a wife. And Brad Finch, as rich a man as you were likely to find in Coldwater, had bought and paid for that divorce. There was a certified check in Jan's handbag for five thousand dollars. A lot of money for a divorce. Or was it? Brad Finch spent more than that on a car.

What was a divorce worth, anyhow? What was a marriage worth? Oh, to hell with it!

She shoved her clothes away with one hand and stretched out on her back on top of the bed. It felt vaguely indecent, lying nude on top of a bed all by yourself in the afternoon. Idly she ran one hand over the front of her body. She touched a breast, thinking that it was definitely nice merchandise, that she had no reason to feel ashamed of her breasts. Were Lily Sue's breasts as nice? They weren't as big, certainly. And they couldn't be much firmer, or much softer, or much nicer to look at.

She closed her eyes. If this were a man's hand, she thought, it would be having the time of its life. And so would she.

She continued to touch her breast, and she felt her nipple go stiff against the palm of her hand. She giggled. No time to be playing games with yourself, she thought.

She laughed aloud.

Things were going to be different, she told herself. There would be plenty of hands to take the place of Jack's hands, plenty of men to do the job much better than it had been done lately. And everything was ready to roll. Soon, very soon, she would have to set the wheels into motion, get the gears grinding away.

On her last trip to New York, when she'd arranged things with Sr. Cojones, the attorney who set up the divorce for her, she'd also made the preliminary arrangements with the three girls. Finding them had been the hard part. A man never has any trouble getting hold of a good call girl, but it's generally a little more difficult for a *woman* to make contact. She had worked things out, though, and the three of them—each perfect—had been located and convinced that her idea was a good one.

Tonight, she thought. Tonight I get in touch with them, and the next day the final arrangements would be made and the essential merchandise purchased. And the day after that they would quite literally get on the road.

She wondered happily what Bradwell Finch would say when he found out how his five grand was being put to use. Not as living money, not at all.

As working capital.

Capital for a fine little business.

A hell of a business. An old one, so they said, but with a new wrinkle. And with plenty of the personal touch added. Maybe they would write her up in *Fortune*. Then again, maybe they wouldn't—although it would triple their circulation overnight.

The hand which had been on her breast moved lower. It coursed over a flat stomach, over a gently rounded belly.

Soon.

Her fingers played. Her eyes stayed closed, her breathing grew heavy, and she slept.

ANDREA MILHOUS AND MARNA Leeds were in their apartment on West 67th Street near the corner of Central Park West. Andrea sat curled up on the couch, a dry Gibson clutched lovingly in one hand. Marna sat in an easy chair with a glass of her own. Andrea was a small brunette with a pixie face, a short haircut and a body that might be described as petite. She reminded some men of Audrey Hepburn. Marna was a blonde with wide blue eyes and a Corn Belt build, big in the hips and breasts and behind, strong in the thighs and arms. She reminded some men of Marilyn Monroe.

Andrea and Marna shared the apartment.

Andrea and Marna were call girls.

Andrea and Marna were also lesbians.

Now this just might seem paradoxical. A lesbian is a girl

who sleeps with girls, and a call girl is a girl who sleeps with men for money. One would think that the twain wouldn't meet, sort of like East and West. In this instance, however, the twain met. Marna and Andrea had the fortunate facility of being able to divorce themselves utterly from their work. The crime syndicate employs certain professional killers who are fine, moral, upstanding family men, pillars in their bourgeois communities—except that four or five or six times a year they travel somewhere and shoot somebody on order. They manage to turn their emotions off in the performance of their business duties, and so did Andrea and Marna.

They slept with men. They earned a marvelous living in this manner.

Then they slept with each other and enjoyed it.

Now it was evening, but this evening they were neither working nor enjoying. They had a visitor, and they were talking with her. The visitor's name was Janice Partridge.

"You know," Andrea was saying, "we've been thinking it over."

Jan raised her eyebrows.

"And it doesn't make too much sense. To us, I mean."

"Why not?"

Marna answered. "We've got a soft touch right here in New York," she said. "We make big money. We have it easy. The fix is in and the police stay away from our door."

"So," Andrea added, "Why leave?"

Jan lit a cigarette. She drew smoke deep into her lungs and held it there for a second or two, then expelled it in a cloud that drifted slowly to the ceiling. She did not say anything. Let them talk it to death, she thought. Then they'd be easier to sell it to all over again.

"The way we understand it," Marna said, "is this. You're going to buy a car. And a trailer."

Jan nodded.

"Then," Andrea went on, "the three of us and some other fly chick are going to hightail it to some nothing town called Coldwater. Where the hell is it, for God's sake?"

"In Kentucky."

"Coldwater," Marna said. "I thought that was a senator or something."

Jan didn't say anything.

"So we go there," Andrea said, "and we turn the trailer into sort of a call house on wheels. We take on all comers for a price that doesn't get close to what we make in New York for turning a trick. And to do this we go live in the middle of nowhere. I don't get it."

"Either," said Marna, "do I."

Jan waited for a moment until she was sure they had nothing more to say. Then she asked them how much they were earning.

"A hundred a night."

"And how many nights do you work?"

"Three or four a week."

"That's three or four hundred bucks a week. Fine. But how much of that do you wind up with?"

"Oh," Marna said. "Well, we have to pay protection. It only stands to reason. Otherwise we could wind up in the tank on Twelfth Street waiting for the spring thaw."

"How much?"

"Half."

"That cuts it down," Jan said. "Right?"

"Right, but—"

"And how much do you save?"

They looked blank.

"You spend a fortune," Jan said. "High rent. Expensive clothes. Dinner out every night. Then—"

"Now wait a minute," Andrea said.

"A girl has to live well—"

"You can't sit and starve—"

"Or wear rags or—"

Jan laughed. "Fine," she said. "You have to live well. And you pay through the nose for it. I'll bet neither of you has saved a penny. Right?"

They hesitated, then nodded almost simultaneously.

"In Coldwater," she said, "you'll make *more* money. You'll get ten bucks a trick instead of a hundred. But you can turn fifty tricks a week with your eyes closed. And you won't have to pay out any fifty percent. You'll pay out one-fifth, and for that I'll take care of the fix and everything else that needs taking care of. That leaves you four hundred a week free and clear. And tax free, incidentally."

She sighed. "That's not all," she said. "The biggest spender in history couldn't go through more than fifty a week in Coldwater. There's nothing to spend it on. No posh restaurants, no fancy stores, and no rent to pay in the trailer."

"But four girls in a trailer—"

"It'll be quite a trailer," Jan said. "Five rooms. A room for each and an office. Listen, I'm not kidding. You work with me for one goddamn year and you'll wind up with fifteen grand free and clear. Does that make sense?"

"I guess so," Andrea said.

"We should put money by," Marna said. "You don't stay young forever. If we saved that kind of money it would be easier to think about retiring."

And that more or less did it. The girls were not very bright, Jan thought. She'd given them the same arguments the first time around and they had agreed for the same damned reason. Intelligent they were not. But they didn't need brains for the kind of work they would be doing.

Which was as it ought to be.

And in fact it was good they weren't too brilliant. This way she would be able to stay in the driver's seat. She controlled them already, for all practical purposes. And it was a pleasant feeling, being able to control people.

Soon she'd be controlling a great many people.

Soon.

She squashed her cigarette, only half-listening while Andrea and Marna hashed over some more dull details. A lot of people were going to find out what a powerful little girl Jan Partridge could be when she felt like it. A lot of people.

The wives, for example. The damned provincial back-biting clique of army wives who had helped to make her life miserable. They would learn a few things when four hot little hustlers from New York moved in and took their husbands away from them—and made a living at it in the process. They'd had their share of laughs when Lily Sue wound up with her own husband. Now it would be her turn to laugh.

And she was going to laugh like hell.

And the husbands—louses just like Jack, and not one of them worth the rotten money the army paid him. She'd take that money away from them, and she'd have them crawling to her on their dirty scabby knees, begging for the chance to plunk down a fast ten bucks for a roll in the hay with her or one of the other girls. And every time she took them for a ride it would be like taking Jack for a ride. Every time she rubbed their noses in dirt she would be getting back at Jack Appleton.

She'd get him, too. Him and that little bitch Lily Sue, that hillbilly with the cat eyes. She'd take her husband right back—only this time he'd have to pay for it. And then she'd throw him back in Lily Sue's face and tell her where to shove him.

And the good citizens of Coldwater. Let them pay, too. Let everybody pay. All of them!

She sighed happily. She stood up.

"I guess that does it," she told Andrea and Marna. "Tomorrow I'll pick up the trailer and the car. The day after that be ready to roll. That means bags packed and everything. I want to get on the road early in the morning. I hate night driving."

"Where will we sit?"

Jan stared.

"When we ride," Marna said. "Do we stay in the trailer or what?"

"In the car," Jan said. "If you rode in the trailer there wouldn't be much left of you when we got there. Trailers have lousy shock absorbers, or none at all."

"How long will we be on the road?"

"Two days. We'll sleep one night on the road, in the trailer. Plug in at a gas station. By the next night we'll be in Coldwater and ready to set up shop."

They walked her to the door. They were in the second floor front apartment of a four-story brownstone. She left them, walked downstairs and out the front door. The night was clear, cooler than the day, but lazily muggy. She stood on the steps for a moment or two, getting the feel of the evening, then crossed the street to hail a cab.

She looked back. Andrea and Marna were in the living room still, and they had forgotten to draw the blinds. They were sitting together on the couch, their arms around each other, and she watched in amusement as they kissed one another.

Dykes, she thought distastefully. A pair of queers. This was what she was carting to Coldwater?

Well, the hell with it. She wasn't going to sit in judgment over them. Although playing games with another girl didn't sound like her own cup of tea, she wouldn't blame another girl for it. It couldn't be worse than letting some swine like Jack Appleton take you for a ride around the block and dump you out in the middle of the street. It wasn't hard to see how a girl could wind up as a lesbian. Men were rats. You stood less chance of getting your teeth kicked in with a girl.

She laughed. Girls were no bargain either, she thought. Girls like the army wives. They were no prize.

But she'd show them.

All of them.

And she'd have her fun at the same time. Not with women, like Andrea and Marna, but with men. They'd pay good money to make love to her and she'd have as much fun out of it as they did. More—because she'd be making a profit on the deal and they'd be paying through the nose.

Fun.

Plenty of fun.

She could hardly wait.

A cab approached. She raised one hand and hailed it. The taxi pulled to the curb and she opened the rear door, slid into the seat. The driver craned his neck around, waiting for her to tell him where to go.

"125th Street and Saint Nicholas," she said.

"Lady, you sure that's where you want to go?"

It was a night for human stupidity. She told him yes, she was sure that was where she wanted to go, and she suggested that he shut his mouth and drive her there. He lapsed into hurt silence and she leaned back, her mind working easily and efficiently.

LIZZIE JACKSON WAS A ten dollar prostitute.

Lizzie Jackson earned ten dollars for going to bed with a man, whereas Andrea Milhous and Marna Leeds received a hundred dollars for more or less the same thing. This monumental difference in price cannot be attributed to the fact that Marna and Andrea were younger or more attractive, since Lizzie was a lovely girl only twenty-five years old. Nor did they give a more spirited performance. Lizzie was an excellent bedroom acrobat, and she took to her trade with vigor and vim.

There was, in fact, quite another reason for the monetary distinction. It was the same reason that Lizzie lived and worked on 126th Street near Saint Nicholas Avenue, which is in Harlem.

Lizzie was a Negro.

"Now that's a point I don't quite understand," Lizzie was saying. "You got a real nice scene building here for yourself. Why do you want to dirty it up with a black girl?"

Jan didn't understand.

"I'm a spade chick," Lizzie said. "A colored gal. In Kentucky they pronounce it *nigger*, the way I hear it. I'll go over down there like Guy Lombardo at the Apollo, baby. Why mess it up?"

"Oh," Jan said. "I see."

"You get it?"

"Uh-huh. But you're wrong."

"Tell me about it."

"What we'll have is something special," Jan said. "Sort of a monopoly. Coldwater doesn't have a red light district or anything of the sort. So we need a house with variety, sort of."

"Something for everybody?"

"That's the idea. I'm a redhead. Marna's a tall blonde. Andrea's a little brunette."

"And I'm a spade."

Jan nodded. "That's right. There are guys around there who come from the smallest towns in the Midwest. They've never been near a colored girl. They think it's something special. You'll be the hit of the house."

Lizzie giggled. "Funny thing," she said. "You get tricks who think just because a gal is brown she's got a brand-new kind of jelly roll. I can lie here stiff as a bored board and they think I'm the greatest thing since Chicago burned."

"That's how it'll be in Coldwater."

Lizzie shrugged. "I can see it," she said. "You talk straight. You make sense. But I don't know if I'll like it down there, baby. It's the South, isn't it?"

"The border."

"Which means it isn't heaven."

"It's not like Georgia."

"Hamburger ain't like fatback. That don't mean it's top sirloin, Jan."

"Is Harlem sirloin?"

Lizzie grinned. "Okay. I'm hip. The bread looks big and I'm sick of New York. I can't make it here any more. My sweet man takes every nickel I sweat for. And I've got a taste for pot that might turn into a horse habit if I hang here long enough. You can count me in."

And that was that. Jan filled the girl in on the rest of the arrangements—time of departure and all—and left the building. She walked down to 125th Street to hail a cab, drawing only a few stares on the way. A white girl in that part of Harlem was not too unusual. Most of the people who noticed her probably thought she was a white hustler in an uptown stable. She didn't care what anybody thought. She grabbed a cab and headed for the hotel, satisfied that she'd done a full night's work.

Of course, she had only given Lizzie part of the story, she realized. What she had said was true enough. It was damned good business to have a Negro girl in the rolling call house. Variety would up their trade considerably.

But that wasn't all.

Because Jan's motives were more then money motives. She wanted to get back at one hell of a lot of people, and

Lizzie would help in that area as well. The narrow-minded army wives, who would be mad enough and sad enough to find out their husbands were playing around with any whores, would be doubly furious if the girl involved was a Negro.

And that was fine with her.

She lit another cigarette in the cab. She smoked thoughtfully and happily. Everything was going to go just fine, she decided. Jack and Lily Sue—and what a hell of a dumb name *that* was!—would get what was coming to them. So would the husbands and wives in the trailer camp. So would the whole rotten stinking stupid town.

A mental picture came into mind. It was a picture of herself standing wide-eyed in the doorway of the trailer she and Jack had shared, staring at the bed where Jack and Lily Sue were making love.

She studied the mental picture. She remembered the expression on Lily Sue's face—it was pure dumb animal passion, and it was obvious that Jack had been putting Lily Sue to her only possible use. The girl would make fine bed company but nothing else. Then too, the same could he said for Jack, when you came right down to it. He was a good basketball player and a damned fine lover, but he had manure between his ears.

She kept the mental picture firmly in mind all the way back to the Commodore. There had been a time when she spent all her waking moments trying to get that same picture out of her head. Then it had hurt too much and she couldn't stand it, couldn't bear the memory.

It was different now.

Much different.

Now she wanted to remember. Now she wanted to prod her memory, because it was a spur to her hatred. And she wanted to hate, wanted her loathing for the two of them to burn with a hard gem-like flame. Only with that hate emblazoned upon the forefront of her mind would she be able to carry through with her plan.

The taxi pulled to a stop. She paid the driver and tipped him, then left the cab and crossed the street. She went straight to her room, undressed, washed up, brushed her teeth and got into her bed. She breathed deeply and slowly in the darkness.

Tomorrow's a busy day, she thought. A very busy day. Tomorrow is a day to cash the check and buy the car and the trailer. It was time to get to sleep, to rest up for the day ahead.

But it was hard to sleep. All the planning and all the talking and all the thinking and all the hating had stirred her both physically and emotionally.

She wanted a man.

She laughed. She needed her sleep, damn it. And in a few days there would be men, loads of men, ton of men. And she wouldn't have to go looking for them because they would come to her.

And they would pay and pay and pay.

Chapter 2

THE LATE-MODEL FORD and the Sturdy Samovar Mobile Home were parked at a gas station outside a nameless village in West Virginia. The proprietor, a chinless man with sparse light brown hair and a rheumy eye, had been a little taken aback when the Ford, loaded with four very attractive girls, had pulled up, asked for a tank of gasoline and a chance to plug in for the night. But, commenting absently that it was "no skin off my nose," he had consented. The trailer was plugged in, taking its electrical supply from the gas station. The proprietor had long since closed up shop and headed for his shack down the road. The sky was dark and a cool snappy wind blew steadily through the hill country.

Night.

And it had been one dilly of a day. One perfect hell of a couple of days, when you stopped to think about it, *if* you wanted to think about it. Jan didn't, really. But there wasn't a hell of a lot else to do. No book that she felt like reading. Nothing on the damned radio but the hillbilly music of which she had gotten sick enough during the time she had spent in Coldwater. Nor was there any companionship available. Lizzie was in her own room, listening on the portable phonograph she had brought, to some modern jazz records which sounded to Jan like traffic noises in Times Square rush hour traffic.

As for Andrea and Marna, they were in the room next to Jan. She wasn't sure what they were doing, and she didn't want to think about it too much, because she had a fairly good idea.

Which left her on her own.

The drive down had been an experience. The whole notion of a little Ford hauling four whores and a trailer was ridiculous at best, and the trip had been weird. Jan did all the driving—if she was going to get killed in a traffic accident, she wanted it to be her own damn fault at least and not someone else's. Andrea and Marna sat in the back seat, talking almost constantly, and alternating between moods of glee in anticipation of the money they would make and misery at the boredom of Coldwater. They seemed to slip from one mood to the next in an instant, and Jan had the persistent feeling that they were a pair of little children incapable of logical thought processes or of a sustained reaction to anything. Lizzie sat in front, next to Jan, and maintained a stony silence for the duration of the drive. The Negro girl was in a mood, an unhappy mood as far as Jan could tell. But at least she was consistent—she was sad all the way, and now she was playing something that was evidently a bopped-up sort of twelve-bar-blues on her phonograph.

A weird thing.

Four whores racing over the countryside.

Four whores.

And that of course was another difficult part. Because, in point of fact, there were *not* four whores in the car. There were *three* whores, plus one girl named Jan Partridge who was going to become a whore in a day or two. No matter how she looked at it, no matter how firmly she told herself that she was essentially the same as Andrea and Marna and Lizzie, she still couldn't help feeling that there was a fundamental difference between them and her. They were prostitutes; they had made their livings selling their bodies to men. She was going to become a prostitute, but as of the moment she was not one.

Which was a difference.

And this little fact, emotionally valid no matter how logically she might attack it, set her on edge. She kept thinking that she was somehow doing the wrong thing, that she was playing the whore without being one, that she was setting herself in a role she did not suit at all.

She wanted to stop the car. She wanted to call the whole show off, to sell the trailer and car to the highest bidder and go back to New York to carve out some sort of life for herself.

This desire came often on the ride. And each time she mastered it, because each time she drew the picture back into her mind of Jack and Lily Sue in bed, Jack and Lily Sue making love. Then the hate welled up in her body, and the urge for revenge surged through her blood, and the other irritating little fact ceased to itch.

Now it was itching again.

The hell of it was, that wasn't all that was itching. Something else was itching, a very special and important part of Jan was itching. And only a man could scratch it.

Christ, she thought. Get a grip on yourself, sweetheart. One more day and the ballgame starts for real. One more day and we can do it all we like and get paid for it. Can't give it away free for nothing. That's a direct violation of union rules. And we ought to have a union, too. The Consolidated Union of Nightwalkers and Trollops.

Sure.

She talked to herself like that, and then the itch almost subsided, and she thought maybe she could go to sleep.

Then something bad happened. Lizzie turned off her record player and went to sleep.

Now this in itself was not so bad. The record player had been no great boon to humanity, and no boon at all to Jan. The problem was something else entirely. With the record player off, Jan could hear what was going on in the room next to her, the room which was housing Andrea and Marna. It was not exactly her idea of Music-To-Forget-About-Sex-By.

It went like this:

Marna: *Mmmmmm!*

(Rustling of bed-clothing, sounds of kissing, soft moans from both occupants.)

Marna: *Do is some more, darling. Right here. That's right. I love it!*

Andrea: *And this? Do you like this?*

(Loud kissing sounds. More moans and groans.)

Marna: *Here! Oh, I can't wait any more. Kiss me—that's right. Oh! Ooooohhh!*

Andrea: *My baby. My darling.*

Marna: *Oh, kiss me! I love it.*

(Loud moans. Bedsprings squealing ever so slightly.)

Marna: *I want to kiss you, too. That's right. Yes, darling. We'll both do it. Yes!*

It didn't stop there, but the hell with it. Jan got the general idea. Jan got a very explicit idea, and the fact that there was no picture to go with the sound did not bother her at all, did not inhibit her reaction to the noise in the least. In some respects radio is infinitely more effective than television, and this seemed to be one of those cases.

It didn't matter that she didn't quite know what the two dizzy dykes were doing. There were several possibilities, and one was worse than the next, and she was going out of her mind.

She had to have a man.

Period. Plain and simple, cut and dried, Jan Partridge had to have a man.

And the sooner the better.

But, even if she gave in to herself and decided to go get a man, where was she going to find one? She couldn't exactly walk the streets until something turned up. In that town they probably had already rolled up the sidewalks anyway. So where did that leave her? She couldn't go knocking on doors looking for a man, could she? That would be bad.

Very bad.

And then, amazingly enough, it occurred to her. It might have been more or less obvious, but it took her a while to come up with it. She could kill two birds with one stone. She could scratch that very persistent itch with an available male, and at the same time she could eliminate that annoying distinction between herself and her employees.

All she had to do was find a man to make love to her—and charge him for it.

That, of course, was the answer. That would unite her in bonds of fellowship with Andrea and Marna and Lizzie, and it would give her a happy little experience to hold and to cherish until they set up shop in Coldwater.

Of course.

Naturally.

The only remaining problem was the choice of a male, and the discovery of a male, and she solved both of those problems in an instant. The only male she knew of was the gas station owner, and she happened to know precisely where he lived. She'd seen him walking to his shack. And, from the look he had given the carload of them, it seemed likely that he'd he more than happy for the chance to knock off a quickie in his cruddy little shack. Unless he had a wife, which somehow seemed unlikely.

Of course he wasn't exactly the ideal lover. He was ugly, and he was kind of old, and he was hardly the most virile-looking specimen Jan had ever come upon. But he was a man, and she could always close her eyes, and anyway he would do in a pinch, and this was one hell of a pinch.

Especially with the sounds that kept coming through the damned wall.

She was half-dressed, half-undressed. As a matter of fact, she was wearing exactly those items of clothing which she did not need. She stood up from her bed and peeled off bra and slip and panties and stockings and garter belt. She put on a tight sleeveless blouse and a tight skirt. After all, there was no point in wearing excess clothing. This way she let the slob see what he was getting, and saved herself time dressing and undressing. It only stood to reason.

Very quietly she let herself out of her room, closed the door, walked to the front of the trailer, opened the door and slipped outside. The night was cool, especially so in view of the way she was dressed. The wind whipped at her and somehow served to excite her just that much more.

Which was fine.

She followed the road around the bend. There was a shack there set back twenty feet or so from the road. In it the gas station man sat in a broken-down chair reading a men's magazine. There was a bed, equally broken-down, in one corner of the room.

It looked inviting.

He was still up, she thought. Well, that was fine. It saved waking him.

She went to the door and knocked on it. Seconds later the chinless man opened the door. If he had had a chin it would have fallen. As it was, his mouth dropped open and he stared.

"Something the matter?"

She smiled. She held her shoulders back so that her breasts were drawn tighter against the front of the blouse. She saw that his eyes were riveted to the V that showed at the top of the blouse.

"Can I come in?"

He couldn't answer. He stepped back and she followed him into the cabin.

"Can I . . . uh . . . help you?"

"Maybe," she said.

"Uh—"

"We're just four poor little girls trying to get across the country," she said, drawling in a burlesque of the local speech. "And we plumb ran out of money. Sure could use some money."

Daylight was beginning to dawn. The idea was striking home. The man looked interested. She decided to get his interest going a little better and unbuttoned the top button of the blouse. It sprang open to reveal the top half of each breast. The man's eyes popped halfway out of his head.

"For ten dollars," she said, "you and I could have fun."

"Ten?"

"Ten," she said, positively.

"Lotta money," he mumbled. He shifted his weight from one foot to the other. "Lotta money. Five might be a leetle more like it. I could let you have five."

She did not want to haggle. The idea of putting out for this negligible excuse for a man had very little appeal, but the whole idea of getting paid for it was lending excitement of its own to the proceedings. She was being the master now. She was exerting the pressure.

She unbuttoned the blouse all the way and dropped it to the floor.

He stared.

Which was only natural. Her breasts stood out true and firm and proud. The nipples were bright with passion, and the rich milky flesh surrounding them could not have looked more inviting.

And he stared.

"Now you listen to me," she said, advancing on him. "You think you could get half this good for ten dollars anywhere else? You ever *see* a pair like these, much less feel them bobbing under you?"

He didn't answer.

"Anytime but tonight," she said, "for ten bucks I wouldn't spit on you. Tonight I need money. I need ten dollars. You think I'm going to come this way again, little man?"

She did not have to say anything more. He went to a cabinet made from an old orange crate, drew out a cigar box and took a ten dollar bill from it. He gave it to her and she bent down to put it in the pocket of her blouse.

Then she took off the skirt. She let him stare, and then she began to swing her hips at him in an imitation, crude but effective, of the bump-and-grind, of a burlesque dancer. He took a step toward her and she backed away.

"Take off your clothes," she said. "Hurry up, get 'em off. Then we'll take a little trip to the moon."

He undressed. There was sparse hair on his bony chest. His flanks were lean, his skin sallow. No man could have looked less inviting, but she went to him, pressing her full breasts hard against his skimpy chest, and she steered him toward the bed. His hands raced over her backside, touching her buttocks. Then they were on the bed.

She did not want to waste time with preliminaries, and she knew instinctively that he would not want to either. For one thing, it had been probably five years since he'd had a woman. He'd probably be pretty short on stamina, and she'd have to take advantage of him while she could.

For another thing, he did not come on like the most sophisticated thing since Max Beerbohm. Subtlety was not his forte, and there was no reason to suspect he'd be more subtle sexually than he was in all other respects.

So they proceeded at once to the main event.

A skilled technician he was not. But this somehow did

not seem to matter. He was a man, and he was there, and he was paying hard-earned money for the privilege of satisfying her own personal desires. She took her pleasure with him, tantalizing him, holding him taut against her, teasing him cleverly.

And then it was over. It happened for him first, as she was afraid it would all along, but she held him in place with monumental energy until she matched his spindly culmination with a fulfillment of her own. They lay together for a moment, and the glow wore off and she thought that now she was a whore, that there was no question about it, that she had crossed a sort of sexual Rubicon and cast a sexual die.

She was a whore.

They got up, feeling unclean, and he looked markedly uncomfortable. It was fairly evident that he wanted her to leave, and she felt much the same way. She had gotten what she'd come for. Despite the total lack of any sexual appeal whatsoever in the man himself, she was thoroughly satisfied. She dressed quickly, buttoning her blouse to the top, and walked to the door.

On impulse she turned in the doorway.

"Give me five dollars more," she said.

He stared at her.

"Cough it up," she snapped. "I was worth it. Give me an extra five."

And, incredibly, he took a worn five-dollar bill from his

cigar box and solemnly presented it to her, an expression of shame on his face. She stuffed it into her blouse pocket and walked back to the trailer.

Power. That was what it was, she decided. That was what made her feel so incredibly good now. Not only the power to make the old skinflint part with ten bucks for the privilege of bedding down with her for a few hectic minutes. More than that—the power to get the scrawny bastard to toss an extra fin into the kitty for the sheer hell of it, just because she asked him to.

Power.

And it felt good.

She let herself back into the trailer. It was silent now; no more sounds came from the room where Andrea and Marna lay sleeping. She wondered idly if they slept in each other's arms. And she laughed softly at the thought.

Her own bed was cool and welcome. She patted the mattress familiarly. You and I are going to be a team, she told the mattress. We'll make beautiful music together.

She laughed again. She stretched out on the bed, settling her head comfortably on the small pillow. Her eyes closed at once and every muscle in her body went magnificently limp. She was exhausted now, physically mentally and emotionally. She was satisfied, and sleep came quickly.

THEY HIT COLDWATER EARLY the following afternoon. Actually it was just another useless little Kentucky town, but for some reason it managed to look far uglier to Jan than to any of the other towns they drove through en route. She approached from the northeast, driving the Ford-cum-trailer the length of Water Street, the main thoroughfare of the town. She glanced at a batch of Coldwater natives. Some of them looked familiar, but she did not know the names of any of them. She saw two unmarried soldiers from MacNamara flirting foolishly with a pair of teenaged Coldwater tramps. That was the sole contact the base had with the town, she thought. The sluts put out for the soldiers. Even the married ones, like Jack.

Well, now the amateur sluts would have some professional competition. She grinned, thinking how that would liven things up. The grin stayed on her face all the way to the trailer camp clear across town.

On the way she pointed out places of interest to the other girls. Andrea and Marna seemed to give a damn about the town, for reasons which she could not comprehend. Lizzie was properly bored; the Negro girl had not said more than *good morning* all day long. For that matter, Jan couldn't really blame her. There was nothing around to get excited about.

The trailer camp was just as she had remembered it. The physical plant itself was much larger than it had to be, which was fine with Jan. That fit into her plans perfectly. All the trailers were grouped at the southern end of the camp in a spirit of togetherness that would have the editors of *Mc-*

Call's in raptures. Jan picked her spot at the extreme northern end of the camp and plugged the trailer's electrical outlet in. That was the perfect spot for them. They were a good fifty yards from the nearest trailer, which would give them plenty of privacy. And at the same time they were about as accessible as you could get.

Not that they would be doing any business to speak of on the trailer plot. That would defeat the whole purpose of the rolling call house. The whole mobility aspect was what made the plan so unique. But, by stationing themselves near the rest of the trailers, they couldn't help get interest aroused. And that would set things up.

Meanwhile she had to establish her contacts. According to her plans, the trailer would be in a different location every night, always within a mile or so of town but never at the same place two nights in a row. This wouldn't fool anybody with a brain in his fat head, but it would give the cops a fine excuse to look the other way once the fix was in. In the meantime, it would keep the cops out of their hair. It took the three-man police force of Coldwater a good month to figure *anything* out, and the county sheriff was even slower.

She went to the bathroom to make up her face, then told the girls to make themselves at home while she went to town for an hour or so. This satisfied Lizzie completely, but Andrea and Marna wanted to know why they couldn't come along. She invented some pleasant explanation to shut them up and cut off further questions. Then she hopped into the car and drove the short distance back to town. She parked the car in a convenient space, got out and started to walk around.

She ran into Clay Duncan in no time at all.

Clay Duncan was a rare bird, the only unattached male who still managed to live in the trailer camp. He had accomplished this simply enough—his wife had run out on him, probably with just cause, and he had never taken the trouble to report this little fact to the authorities. Since he never reported her, and since she never had served any notice of her intention to desert him, they were still officially living together in their trailer—although she did not happen to be there.

He was a tall, rangy man of twenty-eight. He looked as though he should be playing either TV Westerns or first-base for the Yankees—he had that kind of build. His eyes were knowing and cynical, and they widened when they were focused on Jan.

"Well," he said, "I'm damned. No Mexico?"

"I went there."

"So? No divorce?"

"I got the divorce."

He digested this. "But you're back," he said. "How come?"

She let the question pass by. "You're all alone," she countered. "No jailbait handy?"

His grin spread. "Not this minute."

"Must be a lot of trouble," she said.

"What do you mean?"

"This young stuff," she said. "Breaking them in and all. You must get a yen for a woman with a little experience now and then. Somebody who knows her way around a bed."

"You mean you?"

She didn't answer.

"I could go for that," he said slowly, one eye dropping in a wink that managed to be vulgar without half trying. "What the hell—you're not married any more. That means you're fair game."

She laughed at that. Clay had considered her fair game for months, just as he considered every woman, married or unmarried, a valid target. She wondered how much success he had with the other trailer-camp wives.

"That's not exactly what I meant, Clay."

"No?"

"Partly, but not exactly. Clay, what do you do when you can't get ahold of a woman?"

He shrugged. "Buy one. So?"

"And what do the unmarried guys at MacNamara do?"

"Same thing."

"Where do they go?"

"Newport or Covington, mostly. What's the pitch?"

She was all business now, her voice cool and crisp. "I've got three beautiful girls plus myself," she said. "We come fifty miles closer and five bucks cheaper than Newport or Covington. You think we can do any business?"

"What the—"

"It's no joke," she said quickly. "I'm serious."

"You better talk a little slower, honey."

"There are four of us," she said. "Four girls living in a trailer. We're plugged in at number 105 plot at the camp. And we're in business."

"Hustling?"

"Quick thinking, Clay."

"But—"

"A blonde, a brunette, a colored girl and me. The price is ten dollars for a straight trick and it goes up for guys with a vivid imagination. Now do you get the picture?"

He scratched his head. "Jack Appleton's wife," he said. "Old Jack's little woman, the one he played dirty with. I'll be a son of a bitch."

You're one already, she thought. "Interested?"

"How?"

"I figured you'd make a good advertising man," she said. "I want people to know about us. I want a lot of customers. But I don't want to hang out a sign. See what I mean?"

He nodded. "You run a whorehouse in the middle of the camp and you won't need a sign, honey."

"It's a trailer, Clay. They move around."

He nodded again, grinning this time. "Sharper and sharper," he said. "You surprise the hell out of me, Jan."

And of myself, she thought. Aloud she said: "We're in a different place every night. We'll be open for business from eight at night until four in the morning."

"A regular eight-hour day?"

"On the button."

"Keep talking."

"You drop around every morning," she went on. "And I tell you where we operate that night. You spread the word. And the customers come running."

He licked his lips, took a pack of cigarettes from his shirt pocket. He gave one to her, took one for himself and lit both with a windproof lighter. He sighed and blew out a cloud of smoke.

"What's in it for me?"

"What do you want?"

"A percentage," he said. "You'll be raking in a lot of dough. I want a piece of it."

She shook her head.

"It'll be a big pie. You can afford to cut me a little piece of it."

"I'll cut you a different kind of piece, Clay."

He looked at her.

"You've been wanting to get with me for a long time, Clay. You never managed it. Neither did anybody else, anybody but Jack. You can have all you want for free now, sweetheart. All you want."

"I don't know," he said.

"Take a look at the merchandise," she said, posing for him. "Take a long look."

He looked, then grinned cynically. "Nice merchandise, honey. But you can't spend it."

"You can't make love to a dollar bill, either. Take it or leave it, Clay. I can find somebody else easily enough. I picked you because you've got a big mouth. But this damn base is filled with bigmouth guys. I don't need you."

He licked his lips again. "All I want," he said.

"Right."

"I guess I'll take it."

She nodded briefly. "Good enough," she said. "Tonight we'll be on Cemetery Road a mile out of town, if anybody's interested. Drop by tonight yourself. And I'll tell you then about tomorrow."

"Cemetery Road," he said. "One mile out. Probably won't be much business tonight, honey. I can't spread that much word that fast."

"Just use your big mouth."

He grinned, an evil grin. "I hope I'm not the only one with a big mouth, Jan,"

She looked at him.

"You better have a big mouth yourself," he said. "I'm one of those guys with a vivid imagination."

AT SEVEN-THIRTY THAT night Jan hooked up the Ford to the trailer and headed out of town. By that time it was fairly obvious to her that Clay was keeping his half of the bargain. A hell of a lot of the men from the camp managed to pass closer than necessary to the trailer. They all took a good look at whatever girls were in sight, and the looks said plainly enough that they knew how the girls planned to keep body and soul together. It was hard to tell whether the lookers were interested or merely curious. The next week would tell, Jan decided.

When they were about a mile out of town she pulled the Ford and the trailer a few yards off the road. She led the girls back into the trailer, hooking up a battery-powered lantern in each of the rooms. The lanterns didn't illuminate the rooms as well as the regular lights, but unfortunately there just wasn't a plug-in spot sitting out in the middle of nowhere.

"They'll do fine," Lizzie said. "Nobody wants bright lights anyway."

"Some people turn the lights off anyway," Andrea volunteered. "Some men."

"Depends on what the girl looks like," Lizzie said.

For a moment it looked as though Andrea was going to take offense, but Jan changed the subject and the incident was passed off, such as it was in the first place. Jan wondered whether the Negro girl had meant the remark as an insult and decided that she probably hadn't. But that was something she had to watch out for. Tension between any of the girls could ruin the whole operation before it even got off the ground.

They got together in the "office" and sat around waiting for something to happen. It was eight-thirty before anything happened, and all that happened then was that Clay

Duncan arrived to get his hundred-odd pounds of flesh. He and Jan went to Jan's room, where they got undressed and where he explained what he wanted her to do for him that evening.

She had already more or less figured out what he wanted in advance. The act he wanted her to perform might have shocked or disgusted some girls, but her former husband was hardly anything new to her.

As a matter of complete fact, she thought, there was damn little she hadn't been through with Jack. Their sex life together might have been called *Through Krafft-Ebing With Gun and Camera*, she thought. So nothing that Clay could come up with was going to knock her for a loop.

She went through the motions with him, performing her task quickly and easily, neither enjoying it nor getting disgusted. He, however, seemed to enjoy it immensely, and she knew this was one thing his jailbait jollies from town wouldn't do for him. Which meant that she'd have her silly ad man as long as she wanted him. Which was something.

The first cash customer arrived an hour later. He was a boy from town, a kid maybe seventeen or eighteen. Evidently Clay's circle of friends was not limited to army personnel, which was fine with Jan.

The kid came in and stood awkwardly for a minute while Jan asked him whom he wanted. He admitted finally that he'd like to "give the li'l Nigra gal a try," a phrase which didn't exactly send Lizzie into leaps of joy. But they went off together, and Lizzie knocked down the house's first ten-dollar fee.

"Simple," she said. "On and off in less'n a minute. I'll take the young ones any time. They don't tire a woman out so."

There were two more tricks that evening, both of them for Marna. The rest of the girls had no work at all, and for a while Jan thought that morale might drop as a result. After all, eight hours of inactivity can be a drag, especially after two days on the road. Maybe she should have waited a night to open up shop—

But the girls understood, and Andrea, who hadn't had a thing to do all evening, commented that it wasn't at all bad for a first night. At four they turned off lanterns and called it a night, driving back to camp, plugging in the trailer and going to sleep.

Chapter 3

BUSINESS WAS BETTER THE second night. The house take was one hundred and ten dollars, with each of the girls turning at least two tricks. Jan herself turned the only twenty-dollar trick of the evening with a single soldier from the base who had expensive tastes. His idea of fun was a sort of combination deal, and since two special acts were involved Jan gave him the double price. He paid it willingly, and for herself she was amused by the game. It, too, was something she and Jack had done together. And it was even more fun now. She was getting paid for it.

I've been sitting on a goldmine, she thought. I've got something that makes money and I used to give it away for the hell of it. How dumb can you get?

Clay Duncan dropped by again, late in the evening this time. He had his quickie with Jan, then got the location of the next evening's entertainment from her. "Tomorrow'll be a big night," he told her. "It's payday over at the base. You should do one hell of a business. I've been talking the place up, letting the word get around. A lot of the guys are interested."

"They should be."

"They are. But you know how it gets just before pay-day. Most of 'em have been broke. You'd of had a full house tonight otherwise. Tomorrow you'll be turning them away. All four of you girls should be busy for eight hours straight."

"How about the married men?"

Clay shrugged. "Why pay when they can have their own wives for free? Hell, I've been letting the word get out all right. But I think you'll make your money from the single men. A few of the married guys might take a flyer just for the hell of it. That's about all, the way I see it."

"Just keep telling them about it," she said thoughtfully. "Tell 'em how good I am, how good all of us are. Tell them we'll do anything in the world if the price is right." She smiled, more to herself than to him. "I think some of them will be interested. I think some will be damn well interested."

After he left, she stretched out on her bunk before returning to the office. For a moment, with her eyes closed, she thought of the married men, the ones who would make things exciting for her even if they didn't provide the bulk of the revenue.

She thought of one married man in particular.

JACK APPLETON WAS SITTING in the bedroom of his trailer. He heard water running in the bathroom. Lily Sue taking a shower, he thought. He pictured her small, almost dainty body under the spray and he grinned automatically. It was a nice picture. Rounded and pink, a hell of a nice picture.

Lily Sue.

His wife.

His child-bride, really. His bride of three days, married as soon as possible after the telegram confirming the divorce had been received by Brad Finch. Married for good now, he thought. And it was going to be a good marriage, too. One that would last, one that would make him progressively happier instead of driving him nuts as he went along.

It was funny. She was just a kid, a seventeen-year-old hill brat who quit school in ninth grade and couldn't do much more than write her name. And him a college man! It was funny as hell, because he and Lily Sue had a lot more in common than he and Jan had had. Which went to show something or other, anyway.

What it proved was that college only went so far. He was still Arkansas through and through, and Jan was pure New York, and the farther the two of them got from New York the more it showed. She didn't like his friends or his parents or him, when you came right down to the roots of it.

And he didn't like her. She thought she was too goddamn good for the rest of the world. Miss Fancy Pants. A lot of fun in bed, but that was as far as it went. You couldn't live your whole life in bed. You had to spend a little time just sitting around and talking, or go out with a batch of friends, and she was no good when it came to that. Hell, she managed to make him ashamed of himself, as if you were no good if you came from a small town. He was as educated as she was. More, come to think of it—he had his degree and she didn't. But she made him feel like dirt.

Lily Sue was all the difference in the world. For one thing, she'd been a virgin when she came to him, which was more than you could say for Jan. A virgin who learned like lightning, for a fact, but a virgin, nevertheless.

For another, she looked up to him instead of down. As far as she was concerned, he was the greatest, strongest, smartest guy in the world. And her father, liked him, too— not only liked him, but would be in a position to do him a hell of a lot of good once he got out of the damn army. It was a switch, all right. Most of the townies hated most of the army people sight unseen, but Bradwell Finch could see beyond the cover and tell what a man was like. He knew Jack and Lily Sue were the same kind of people, that Jack could fit in fine in a town like Coldwater. And as soon as he got out of the army they'd settle down right there. And Brad Finch would give him a better job than he'd get anywhere else, with a piece of the business coming his way if he was any good at it.

His friends liked Lily Sue, too. And she liked them. And it was sure as hell a nice switch to have a social life, to sit around and talk to people instead of hiding your wife in the closet and hiding your friends in another closet because they just plain didn't get along. It made a difference. It let a man feel as though he had a full life, not two half-lives starved for oxygen and fighting each other to stay alive.

He thought about these things, and about other things, and then he stopped thinking because the water stopped running in the bathroom and a few seconds after that the door opened and Lily Sue emerged.

He caught his breath and stared at her. Her pink body was wrapped in a pink towel that failed to cover her too well. The tops of her breasts were visible over the top of the towel, and the tops of her thighs were visible under the bottom of the towel, and all in all she looked too good to be true.

"Come here," he said. He held out his arms for her and she came to him. His hands went under the towel and caressed her, playing eager games with her warm body. He kissed her and she returned the kiss.

Then suddenly she pulled away. "Well," she said. "What do you think of it?"

"I think it looks good. Now lie down and let me fool with it."

She giggled. "Not me, silly. The news."

"What news?"

"About her."

He did not understand at all. "You better pull back and start over, Lily Sue. You lost me around the last turn."

She sighed. "The big news," she said. "About Jan."

"Huh?"

"You mean you didn't hear? I thought—"

"Hear *what*, for Christ's sake?"

She sighed again, then sat down beside him on the bed. "Your old wife is back in town," she said.

"Jan?"

"You got any other old wives?"

"I don't get it," he said, scratching his head. "She must be looking for more money. Well, she came to the wrong place. She won't get a nickel from me or from your old man. That divorce is good and legal and she can't make any trouble one way or the other. She can just go to hell for herself."

"She's looking for money, Jack. But that's not how."

"I still don't get it."

Lily Sue sighed again. "She's here in a trailer," she said. "Her and three other girls. Three fancy girls from New York. They're starting a cathouse."

"What the hell!"

She went over the situation briefly, explaining the operation that Jan and the girls were building up. She told him that they were using the trailer as a cathouse on wheels, told him what they were charging and how they were working things. His eyes went wider and wider the more she talked. His mouth dropped open and he had a staggered look on his face by the time she was through.

"Well, I'm damned," he said. "I'm damned."

He looked at Lily Sue. "Maybe she's showing her real self," he said. "Maybe she's just a natural-born whore from the word go. Maybe that's it."

"Maybe."

"How'd you hear about it?"

She shrugged. "Wasn't much way to *help* hearing about

it. I keep my ears open, Jack. I hear things. And you must be the only man in camp who doesn't know. Everybody's talking about her."

"Nobody told me," he said. "Maybe they figured I knew. Or maybe they thought I wouldn't want to hear about it."

"I guess."

He yawned, then reached for her again. "Hell with her," he said. "Let her take on the whole world. Hell with her."

"How come she came here, Jack?"

"Damned if I know. Wants to make some money, I guess."

"I don't think so."

"No."

Lily Sue set her jaw. "I think she wants to make trouble," she said. "Trouble for us. I think she wants to get even with me for taking you away from her. And to get even with you for leaving her high and dry."

He thought about that. "Nothing she can do," he said.

"She can try."

"Won't do her any good."

"No good at all," Lily Sue said. "She gets near you and I kill her. I swear to God I will kill her!"

Jack stared. His bride meant every word she was saying and it bowled him over to see the fury and determination blazing in her eyes. She was some woman.

"Let's forget her," he said, snatching the towel away from Lily Sue. "Won't need to kill her," he went on, caressing the young freshness of her breasts. "There's not a thing she can do. Not a thing in the world."

He kissed the breasts gently and watched the play of expressions across Lily Sue's face, watched her eyes turn from fury to relaxation, from relaxation to desire, from desire to flaming passion.

She moaned.

"Forget her," he whispered, breathing heavily. "We're all that matters. You and me, we matter. And that's all."

He pushed her down on the bed. He ran his hands over her body, desire building up within him so powerful he couldn't withstand it. She welcomed him as he filled the rich sweetness of her with the brutal force of his love.

PAYDAY WAS PAYDAY IN more ways than one. It was, first of all, the day an impressive number of men at MacNamara Base received their money. Since the average GI was flat broke by the time payday rolled around, this greatly changed the base's financial picture.

It was also payday for Jan, in that the operation really started to pay off that evening. Clay had been right—the interest was there and all that was needed was a little cash to start things rolling. Her trailer was wheeled into place a half-hour early, ready for business in its new location. And at a quarter to eight the first customers rolled around. Four men from the base drove up, stopped to look at the trailer, then drove on a ways and parked. They came back on foot, and the look in their eyes when they saw the four girls showed that they were loaded for bear.

Andrea, Marna and Lizzie each wound up in a room with one of the soldiers. The fourth waited in the office with Jan, explaining that he certainly didn't want her to take offense, that he found her most attractive but that he had a preference for blondes.

Jan grinned. "Marna's worth waiting for," she told him. "But she'll be here a long time. You can give her a whirl next week, you know."

"I thought—"

"I'm lots of fun," she said. She didn't want to turn a trick particularly, but this was a challenge and she couldn't help responding to it. "I'm one hell of a lot of fun. Why wait when you can have that fun right now?"

"I got a preference for blondes," he repeated lamely, grinning idiotically.

She walked over to him. Her agile fingers worked cleverly and got the results they wanted.

"You got a preference, all right," she told him. "But why does it have to be just for blondes? Can't a little old redhead get into the act?"

From there on it was no contest at all. The soldier followed her to her room and he had his hands on her before the door was closed. He was in too much of a hurry to bother undressing. He tossed her down on the bed, and in an instant he was with her.

She hadn't wanted a man at the beginning. She hadn't even felt much like turning a trick. Originally she was interested in the soldier only as a challenge, only as a man who was waiting for another girl and whom she could dominate with the force of her own sexual attractiveness. Now, however, she did not have to pretend to be excited. By now she herself was burning with passion, and her body rolled and her nails dug through his shirt.

It was over very quickly. Then they rose from the bed and she straightened her clothing. It was only then that she remembered to collect her ten-dollar fee. She'd been so excited that the money had slipped her mind.

Marna was a little annoyed when she discovered that her trick had already been taken care of. But on that particular evening she had nothing to complain about. From eight o'clock on the tricks rolled in in a steady stream, with more work than the four girls could handle. There was no let-up until well after midnight, and some men continued io roll in clear through to three-thirty in the morning. At a quarter-to-four Jan closed up shop and headed the trailer back to the parking place. She put all the money in the small safe she had had installed in the trailer, entered each girl's earnings in an account ledger, and sat at her desk, lost in thought.

So much money!

And so much fun, for that matter. The base itself had not been the sole supplier of clientele that evening. There was one married man in crew—a fellow whom she recognized but whose name she did not remember. He wasn't a trick of hers—Andrea got him—but that didn't make much difference. He was a customer. The first blow against the army wives had been struck. Inevitably, there would be other customers. Trailer-camp husbands would ruin their budgets cheating on their wives. And she would turn a neat profit on the deal.

It was working out fine. She closed up the office and went to bed, feeling strange now, sleeping in the bed where she had earned so much money and satisfied so many men so recently. But it was a good bed, and she didn't mind it at all.

She didn't even mind the sounds that came through the wall from the room where Andrea and Marna were making love. She listened for a moment two, and she was mildly amused.

Then she fell asleep.

"IT'S BETTER THIS WAY," Andrea said.

"What way? We're not *doing* anything, silly." Marna giggled. "Besides, I don't believe there's a better way."

"That's not what I mean. I mean working for Jan. I thought it was going to be a come-down after New York."

"Oh. I thought you liked the idea."

"She talked me into it," Andrea said. "Same as she talked you into it. I was worried. I mean, the idea of going with that many guys in a night. In New York it was one guy a night for a lot of money. I thought it would be a big drag. I thought it would be horrible. But you know, in a way it's better."

"More money," Marna said.

"That's just part of it. But you said it right there, sugar. Of course every night won't be like tonight. This was something kind of special. Payday, Jan said. No, it's not just the money. We did okay that way in New York."

"What, then?"

Andrea stroked her chin. "I don't know exactly," she said. "But when you're with that many men all in a row it's like you're not really doing it at all. It's a machine, you know? You just lie there and do what you're supposed to do and that's all there is to it. Nothing more."

Marna was nodding. "And with one man it's different," she chimed in.

"Uh-huh. Sometimes you would have to be with him the whole night, and you'd make love lots of times, and it was like giving him part of yourself. You know what I mean? All we give these soldiers is five or ten or fifteen minutes. Then they can go to hell on a broomstick for all I care. It's just better. That's all."

They were both nude, both on the bed. Marna was lying down, her face against the pillow, her bottom pointed vaguely at the ceiling. Andrea sat on the edge of the bed. She was touching Marna in a strangely detached manner, an almost asexual manner. They had showered and they were relaxing before bed, with Andrea smoking a cigarette. Soon they would make love, but for the time being they were merely talking.

Marna rolled over onto her side. She yawned hugely and stretched like a large fat cat at dawn. Andrea's hand moved automatically and continued its gentle fondling.

"A funny thing happened," Marna said.

"Tonight?"

"Uh-huh. There was this trick I had. A weird one. You'll never guess what he did."

"What?"

"What we do. Except it was different."

"Tell me about it."

"It was funny," Marna said. "Do you remember that one trick I had, he came in all by himself?"

"That's a bright description—"

"I wasn't finished. A real thin kid with light brown hair and glasses. Skinny. And shy, like it was his first trip and he was scared one of the cats might scratch him."

"I don't remember him."

Marna shrugged. "It doesn't matter, I guess. Anyway, he was the one. An odd one. He didn't even want to take off his clothes."

"He wanted to make love with his clothes on?"

"Let me finish. He didn't even want to go with me, actually. The first thing he did was make me take all my clothes off. Then he took his belt and handed it to me. He wanted me to give him a beating."

"I've had guys like that. Masochists. It's not so weird. I'm not saying he wasn't kind of an oddball, but you get them all the time."

"Let me finish, will you, Andy? This one was different. I stood there holding onto the belt, see, and he got down on his knees in front of me and told me to start slugging him with the belt. So I started to give it to him. And then the funny part came in. He put his arms around me and started to kiss me while I was belting him."

"Kiss you?"

"Uh-huh."

"Oh," Andrea said.

"It was the funniest damn thing. There he was, working away, and there I was lashing the stuffing out of him. And you know it was funny. I mean, I don't get a thing from a man most of the time. But this way it was different."

Andrea looked alarmed.

"Take it easy," Marna said. "You got to let me finish before you blow up, okay? I got a little excited for two reasons. For one thing, with what he was doing I could close my eyes and pretend it was you. See?"

Andrea nodded.

"And another thing. While he was doing it, I was knocking him silly with the belt. He was a man, see, and I was pounding him one with the belt. That helped get me excited. It got so I was really hitting hard. The poor jerk had welts all over his back by the time he was done."

"Don't feel sorry for him," Andrea advised. "That's what he wanted."

"Maybe. But it was funny."

"You didn't enjoy it, did you?"

Marna laughed aloud. "He was a man, for God's sake! What do you think I am?"

"I just wondered."

"I got a little excited," Marna said. "That's all. A little excited. But not like with you." She grinned slyly. "You know what? I think you're jealous."

Andrea didn't deny the charge. Instead she rolled Marna over onto her back and crouched beside her. She took a deep breath, her hands on Marna's shoulders, her eyes boring into the blue eyes of the busty blonde.

"So I'm jealous," she said. "So I'm going to make you feel so eager now that you're going to forget all about every man in the world. Any objections?"

"None."

"Then lie very still," she whispered. "Tonight it's going to be my turn all the way. You can't do a thing. You've got to lie there while I send you around the world. Understand?"

"I understand."

"You just lie there," she repeated. "You just lie there and don't move a muscle. I'm going to make you see stars."

"Andy—"

"Close your mouth, honey. And your eyes. Just relax and see how good everything is."

Andrea watched the blonde girl go quietly limp. Then she leaned over her and pressed her mouth to Marna's mouth. She kissed steadily, carefully, and Marna's mouth opened to admit her tongue. She kissed Marna on her warm red mouth for several minutes. Then she moved lower, her lips pressing to the soft skin on Marna's throat, gliding over the smoothness. Marna purred like a kitten and she smiled to herself, pleased with the effect her caresses were having upon the blonde.

She kissed Marna's shoulders.

Then her breasts.

Such beautiful breasts, she thought. Such magnificent, full breasts. Not like her own breasts at all. Her own were small and she didn't like them—she had never liked them. But Marna's were different. Marna's were big and rich and delicious, and she loved to hold them, loved to kiss them, loved to touch them and caress them.

And Marna liked it, too.

Andrea kept kissing.

Andy's smile spread. It was much better this way, she thought. Better to be in Coldwater than in New York. In Coldwater, the two of them were alone, completely alone, two gay girls in a very straight world. In New York, the town was crawling with dykes, and although she knew full well that Marna wouldn't cheat on her, she was a jealous person by nature. She couldn't help worrying. Here in Coldwater there was absolutely nothing to worry about. Marna was hers and only hers.

And no more of the same kind of worrying when Marna spent the night with a man. Here Marna would have ten or twenty men a night, or thirty even, and it wouldn't make a bit of difference to her. None of the men would spend much time with her, while in New York when one of them had her all night long it was too much for Andy to take.

As far as that one weirdo went, she couldn't care less now. Hell, she herself had been occasionally excited with a man. It didn't mean a thing. Marna was gay through and through, and Marna belonged exclusively to Andy, and that was all that mattered. The rest could fly a broomstick to hell.

She blazed a trail of kisses down Marna. Tonight she was going to be a tease, a tantalizer. Tonight she was going to have fun.

Then she began.

The whole world dipped and swayed. The trailer rocked like a cradle and the world turned upside down. She kissed Marna again and again, and Marna tangled desperate fingers in her hair and almost tugged it out by the roots, and it got better and better until it exploded.

Then they slept.

LIZZIE COULDN'T SLEEP.

It was quiet now. No more love-and-chatter from the Twisted Twins. No more nothing. Just soft sounds on the record player and a cool wind making noises outside the window.

That was all.

Just dirt and filth. Just men who were more willing to pay for the privilege of making love to a woman whom they regarded as inferior. Just men who treated her like slime—and how wrong were they, really?

She was slime. Cool green slime, cool as the wind but dirty clear through. No good at all. Good in bed because she knew the moves and it was just like dancing when you knew how, just like playing checkers, just like anything where you could fit into a quiet groove that didn't mean a thing to you.

Nothing meant a thing.

Nothing at all.

And it wasn't so groovy that way. It wasn't so crystal-cool when you were turned off all the time, when you never felt a thing, when life was just listening to a record and eating a meal and never having anything happen that you could feel was the least bit important.

Not cool any more.

Just cold.

Cold as ice. Cold as death.

Cold.

That was the bad part. There were times when it was better not to feel anything—when there was nothing good to feel, when you were dirt through and through with no goodness to you, when everybody treated you like dirt and used you for their public doormat. At times like that it was better if you couldn't feel anything, if you could go through life turned emphatically off because there was nothing to turn on to.

But you couldn't live that way. You couldn't call that a life, not twenty-four hours a day of it and seven days a week of it and fifty-two weeks a year of it. It was something that didn't make sense that way, because when you were turned off you were not entirely alive, were not alive at all in fact, and you were nothing but a hibernating bear, never going to wake up.

You might as well die.

Die.

Well, why not die? Why not take out a razor blade and open up her veins and bleed all over their damned trailer? Why not get thoroughly stiff, why not end it and to hell with it and good-bye?

Why not?

Because death was a long gig, she thought. Because death lasted even longer than life and couldn't be a hell of a lot better. Because she was afraid, and because she wasn't quite tired and dragged enough yet to give up.

Besides, if you were going to do yourself in you had to do it up brown. Like that painter, that Modigliani. He was a junkie and a juicer and a hell of a painter, and he got tuberculosis and died of it, and then his mistress decided to do herself in. Her parents screamed on her when she went to live with the cat, so she went back to their home and they were so goddamned phony-happiness glad to take her in, and she went up to her room and went out on the balcony and took a jump to the courtyard and splattered herself into little pieces.

That was the way to do it. That said something, it moved, it swung, it fit. But when a whore opened her veins it didn't mean a thing. It was just another dead whore in another deadly cathouse, and there wasn't a person in the whole cold world to give a hoot.

So no death.

But she was turned off. And when you were turned off, there was only one sensible thing you did.

You turned on.

She sighed, because she had decided not to do this for awhile but there didn't seem to be any choice. Then she opened her little suitcase and rummaged through it until she found the box. It was a small Japanese box that had a trick you did to open it, sliding certain panels. She did the trick and the box opened. She studied the contents thoughtfully.

Five little brown cigarettes. Five little slips of paper, five little cylinders with twisted ends.

Five trips to the moon. Five turner-onners, five nights when she could stay alive without feeling like death.

And what was she going to do when they were gone?

She laughed. Buy more, she thought bitterly. Buy more, and take more trips to the moon, and then one day decide to hell with it, let's turn on to something big, let's make the major leagues. And then buy white stuff instead of brown stuff, capsules instead of paper tubes, stuff that you cooked and injected instead of smoking.

Like heroin.

But not yet. Not yet, because there were five little sticks left and each was good for one more jaunt along the tread-mill to oblivion. The rest would come later. Give it time and it would come, inevitably.

She took out one of the marijuana cigarettes, closed the box and returned it to her suitcase. She put the cigarette to her lips and took a deep breath which she held for a moment, then let out slowly. Finally she scratched a match and lit the cigarette, sucking hard on the stick, dragging acrid smoke deep into her lungs.

She held the smoke down as long as she could. Then she blew it out the window. An automatic precaution, probably unnecessary since the other girls could smell the stuff all day long and not know what it was.

Then another drag. You had to keep your lips open so that you sucked in a mixture of air and smoke, and you had to take it straight to the lungs, not like with a straight where you just smoked and inhaled. Pot was special. There was an effect you were reaching for, and a regular ritual went with it.

She smoked the joint all the way down. Then she took the small butt, the roach, and tucked it into the hol-lowed-out end of a regular cigarette so that she could smoke it as well. By that time it was working, the pot was making her blood boil and her brain was crystal cool and moving like happy. She finished the roach and put out the cigarette. Then she put a Monk record on the box and stretched out on her bed. The room was better now, and the bed was clean and so was she.

Everything was all right.

Chapter 4

A WARM LAZY AFTERNOON. A patch of clouds in the sky, but none of them getting in the way of the hot summer sun. The sun burned down on Coldwater, and people reacted to the heat just as lizards react to the cold. Their metabolism slowed down.

Jan passed men who sat on their porches, rocking quietly in ancient rocking chairs, sitting and smoking or drinking in the shade. She looked at the people she passed and she noticed how they looked back at her. They stared now. They knew what she was, what sort of business she was running, and their knowledge showed in their faces, in their glances.

This pleased her. Two weeks, two brief weeks and the whole town knew about Jan Partridge's trailer. Two weeks and the whole place was buzzing. The knowledge was reflected not only in the eyes of the citizens of Coldwater but in the gross receipts of the trailer itself. Business was as good as she could want it to be. The money came in steadily and none of the girls had any complaints. Sometimes they acted a little strange, but she didn't really care about that. They did their work well enough. They seemed happy, and the customers sure as hell seemed happy, and that was all that counted.

She herself was definitely among the happy ones. While the base remained the chief source of income, the trailer camp and the town were beginning to hum. Several businessmen from town, small store-owners and such, were customers. Half a dozen married men from the camp had already been there more than once, and another dozen or so had made their initial visits. She had a commodity for sale and nobody seemed able to resist it. Friction would be brewing soon in the camp and in the town. All the seeds were sown. It was only a matter of time.

She stopped at the drugstore, picked up a newspaper from the stand outside and dropped a nickel in the cup provided. The druggist avoided her eyes—he had been up to the trailer, and according to Andrea's rather startled report he had ideas which his own wife would certainly have been unwilling to satisfy. She flashed him a sadistically knowing grin and headed on down the street. She was supposed to meet Clay at Bauer's Luncheonette around three. Clay already knew where the trailer would be parked that night—not that she expected much business; it was a Monday night, and on top of that, both Andy and Marna were on their monthly vacations. But she wanted some special information from Clay.

She laughed. Clay would do anything she asked him to do. The sex bit, in return for which he acted as her agent, had turned neatly until she was quite firmly in the driver's seat.

It had been another milestone along the road to power, designed more than anything else to establish their position so that he enjoyed no power over her. And it was simple enough. She had merely waited until an opportune evening, at which time she informed Clay that she wasn't going to let him make love to her that night.

"Come back tomorrow," she told him. "I don't feel like it tonight. Maybe I will tomorrow."

He had been angry. "What the hell," he said. "You said all I want whenever I want it."

"I changed my mind."

"Dammit, you can't do that!"

She had smiled sweetly. "If I do," she said, "what in hell can you do in return?"

"You can find yourself a new ad man, honey."

She left it at that. He went away without what he had come for, and for the rest of the evening she told all her customers where she would have the trailer parked the next evening. When he came around the following night she was doing business as usual. "See?" she had said. "I don't need you at all."

That set things up. From that point on she let him possess her when she felt like it, making a point of passing him up every few nights to keep him on the hook. In return for this he did more than advertise—he acted as her agent, reporting on attitudes on post and in the trailer camp, relaying messages for her and otherwise making himself useful as a liaison officer between herself and the world.

She went into Bauer's, found a booth near the rear and ordered a pair of rare hamburgers and a mug of black coffee. The kid who brought her order gave her a long and wistful stare that peeled the clothes from her. She was amused.

"Forget the whole thing," she told him. "You couldn't possibly afford it."

"I can manage ten bucks," he mumbled, hurt. "If you're worth that much."

She laughed. "That's not the only thing," she said, her voice coated with sugar. "There's a law in this state. I could get in trouble."

That crushed him. She watched him walk away with his young pimply face hanging out and she laughed. Maybe I'm a sadist, she thought. I get a hell of a kick pushing their faces in it. Maybe there's something wrong with me.

She sighed. No, there was nothing wrong with her. She wanted to get even and that was all there was to it. And why shouldn't she? The town had given her the royal barbed shaft, and the wives had twisted the shaft around a little, and Jack had rammed it in farther, and the rotten little witch named Lily Sue had broken it off inside her.

Why shouldn't she want to get even? It only made sense, good sense. Damn good sense. They had it coming, and they deserved to lap up every bit she dished out at them. To hell with every one of them!

She was working on her second hamburger when Clay sat down across from her. He took a pack of cigarettes out and offered it to her. She took one and let him light it for her. After a long drag she looked him in the eyes.

"Okay," she said. "Let's have it."

"I don't know where to start."

"Any place is good enough."

His fingers played drums on the tabletop. "First of all, you can expect a visit any day now."

"From you?"

"From Ernie Perkins, beloved and efficient police chief of Coldwater. He finally decided to pay attention to the complaints."

"We're not within city limits," she said. "Does that make any difference?"

"Not to Ernie. You're a civic nuisance. That's the way he'll look at it, although most of the men around here think you're a public benefactor. But he's been getting complaints."

"Where from?"

Clay shrugged, then held his hands wide.

"From everywhere?"

"Damn near. From the women in town, ranging from the church groups and back again. I don't know—maybe they're afraid their husbands will find out what a real fling is like. And from the wives at the trailer camp, naturally. They don't like you, honey."

"They never did," she told him. "I don't like them a hell of a lot myself. But Ernie Perkins never gave much of a damn about the military, the way I remember it. He shouldn't much care what they say."

"He doesn't, but it's more fuel on the fire. Or fat on the fire, or something. He should be around to see you. I'm not sure how he'll handle it. If you're lucky he'll get in touch with you in private. If you're unlucky it'll be worse. Messy."

"A raid?"

"Something like that. It wouldn't be bad from his point of view. He'd have a chance to lock up one hell of a lot of soldiers. Ernie doesn't exactly love soldiers. And neither do the fine citizens of Coldwater. They'd approve."

She thought it over, smoked the cigarette. "I'm not worried about Ernie," she said. "I can take care of him. But a raid might be bad. I'll beat him to the punch and go see him this afternoon. That'll take care of things."

"Bribe him?"

"You know a better way to get around a cop?"

"I guess not," he admitted.

"So to hell with Ernie," she went on. "There's one kind of cop it's pretty tough to fix. The MPs. They know about me?"

"They knew the day you opened. They're louses, but they keep their ears to the ground all right. Thorough louses, you might say. You can forget about them. *They* sure as hell don't get any of the complaints. And they know damn well that their discipline problems go way up when there's no house in the area. All the army cares about is giving each kid a kit so he doesn't come home with a disease. That's all."

She nodded. "That's what I thought. Okay, that takes

care of that part of it. I'll see Perkins today. Now tell me what's new in the camp."

"You ought to know. You live there."

She laughed, pleased. "I don't exactly feel like a member of the in-group," she said. "They leave me out of things. I miss most of the neighborhood back-fence gossip."

"Maybe it's because you don't keep the same hours as they do," he suggested.

"Maybe. Go on—tell me about it."

"Not much to tell, honey. Bud Reagan been coming to your place?"

"Once. Why?"

"His wife heard about it. Or at least the word is that she heard about it. She went back to see her mother—a sort of vacation. She'll probably be back in a few days when she cools off a little. But she gave Bud a black eye that'll take that long to wear off."

"That's good news. What else?"

"The rest of the wives wish you would take arsenic and die. That's not news, is it?"

"It never was."

"They wish it more than ever," he said. "Every last one of them. Of course, none of them are willing to believe that *their* hubbies would have anything to do with you or your girls. But they seem a little more worried than they try to let on."

"Good."

"They're even getting up a committee. That's how the protest got to Ernie, as a matter of fact. An Army Wives Committee designed to abolish mobile whore houses. And I'll give you three guesses who's heading that committee."

"Do I need three guesses?"

"One ought to do it, I guess. She's sort of a relative of yours. By marriage, that is. That ought to be some kind of a relationship."

"It is. We hate each other. Well, I'm glad I'm getting under her skin. But what in hell is she mad about? I haven't seen Jack buzzing around the trailer. Is he getting interested?"

He shook his head. "If he is," he said, "I don't know about it. He never even talks about you, or about the trailer. It's as if he didn't know you were there."

She took another cigarette to cover her disappointment. Well, it was only to be expected. It was going to take some real work to get to Jack. But it was only a matter of time. She would get to him, and she would settle with him. Time would tell.

She shifted gears.

"There's somebody at the camp named Will Something-or-Other. A tall drink of water with a low forehead and yellow hair. You know who I mean?"

"Might be Will Taylor."

"That's it. You know much about him?"

He shrugged again. "I don't know him too well. Pretty nice guy, far as I can tell. Doesn't talk much."

"What's his wife like?"

"Skinny gal. Not much on looks but a pretty nice kid. Quiet. Hell, I don't even know her name."

Of course not, she thought. You don't want to make her, so why should you know her name?

"He was up at the place," she said. "He was with Marna, my blondie. She said he really seemed to like her, more than just to roll around with. Kind and thoughtful and that baloney."

"Uh-huh."

"So I want to know more about him," she went on. "And about his wife, too. And you can let him know that Marna has a thing for him. She likes him a lot. Sort of let him know that."

He looked surprised. "Hell," he said, "I thought you told me she was a dyke."

"I did."

"Then—"

"And she is," she finished. "But you don't have to tell that to Willie Boy, or to anyone else. Just let him think she's in love with him. It ought to get interesting."

ERNEST PERKINS WAS AS good a police chief as the town of Coldwater wanted him to be. He enforced the laws that were supposed to be enforced and ignored the ones that were laws in name but not in fact. He was a practical man, and Coldwater could not have wanted a better chief of police.

He could have been better. He could, for example, have arrested Luke Trumbo any day of the week for booking horses and writing numbers. The fact that he didn't do this was not a result of the fact that Luke sent him a check for a few hundred bucks every Christmas. This was incidental. The primary reason was that Coldwater *wanted* somebody to book horses and write numbers, and that a police chief who failed to take this into account would find himself rewarded with sudden and inexplicable loss of employment.

He could have made dozens of arrests for drunkenness, but you do not do this in a small town. Small towns are more tolerant of their local drunks than are large metropolitan centers. The man who is drunk one night is over for dinner the next night, and there's no point in keeping him in jail in the interim.

So Ernie Perkins did the job he was supposed to do. He rode herd on the servicemen without stopping them from spending in Coldwater the money essential to Coldwater's economic survival, such as it was. He caught thieves periodically if they were sufficiently slow-footed, he swelled the coffers of the town treasury by ticketing out-of-state cars which may or may not have been speeding, and he did his bit to calm down the high spirits of rebellious youth on such festive occasions as Halloween, the Fourth of July, New Year's Eve, and any and every Saturday night.

He was a relatively decent sort of man. He lived with a wife and two children in a white frame house with a basement, a garage, a front porch and a mortgage. He earned four thousand two hundred and fifty dollars per year, plus perhaps another five hundred dollars for what a reformer would nastily term graft. He was a paunchy man of forty-eight, a cigar-smoker and a moderate bourbon-drinker, a lousy shot with pistol or rifle but a good man in a fight.

He was at his desk in his office when Janice Partridge walked in. She came unannounced, and no one saw her enter. Which, she knew, was just as well.

Ernie Perkins agreed that it was just as well.

"I've got a complaint to make," she said.

He looked at her.

"There's a whorehouse in town," she went on. "Four New York prostitutes are working in a trailer. It's a real local eye-sore and something ought to be done about it."

Ernie opened the top drawer of his desk and found a cigar. He smelled it, rolled it between his fingers, bit off the tip and spat it in the vague general direction of his green trapezoidal wastebasket. He put the cigar in his mouth, scratched a long wooden match on the underside of the desk and lit the cigar. He smoked.

"The way I heard it," he said slowly, "you run the place."

"That's right."

Ernie sucked on the cigar. This woman was an odd one, all right. He'd just about made up his mind to have a talk with her and find out what exactly was going on, and here she was turning herself in. There were any number of things he might have said to her at this point, but he had played a great deal of poker in his day. It was her turn to bet or fold. He didn't say a word.

"I run the place," she said finally. "I'm the madam. And I want to stay open."

He thought about that. "Some people," he said, "want to see you close up."

"I know."

"And you want to stay open?"

"That's right."

He nodded. "You trying to make some sort of a point? Or are we just talking about the state of the union?"

"I'll make plenty of points," she said, her eyes still locked with his. "Let's talk about what you're making. You making much, chief?"

"You mean money?"

She nodded.

"I get by," he said. "I eat okay."

"On four grand a year?"

"Forty-two fifty," he corrected. "I got a raise last year. The council decided I was doing a good job."

"That's a big salary?"

He took another puff of the cigar. It looked as though she was about to offer him a hundred dollars to leave her alone, and she was making a big production out of it. He was trying to make up his mind what to do. It occurred to him that he could take the hundred and shut her down anyway, but that wasn't fair. He didn't like to cheat.

So the question was more whether or not it was worth a hundred to let her stay open. Or two hundred, say. There was no question but that he could use the money. A hundred dollars made a difference when you earned less than that for a week's work and not much more after two week's work when the government got through cutting its share out of the pie. So it was a ticklish problem. He had to balance the hundred dollars on the one hand against the complaints on the other.

The army wives he could ignore, like as not. Nobody who voted paid them any mind. And the church groups were always complaining about something or other anyway. There were only a few complaints that carried any real weight and he could probably dodge them without too much trouble.

So it was mainly a question of how much she was going to offer.

"It looks like you're about to come up with a bribe," he said bluntly. "In which case you don't have to fence around like a ballet dancing fool. Come out and say what you're planning on saying or go somewhere else."

She laughed appreciatively. "You say what you mean," she said. "That's good."

"You oughta do the same."

She grinned. "All right," she said. "I want to stay open. And unless I'm way off the track you wouldn't mind making extra money. If I'm off the track I'm through anyway, since you can shut me up any time you damn well please. Right? So I have to make you an offer. Something that'll work for both of us. It's not an offer you boost. It's a set price and you can take it or leave it."

"How much?"

"One hundred dollars," she said.

He pursed his lips. The price was what he had thought it would be. It seemed small enough, but there was always the fact that he could shake an extra hundred out of her now and then if he wanted to. And that he could close her down the minute he felt like it and keep the money—if the pressure came too hard and too fast.

"One hundred dollars a week," she repeated. "That more than equals your salary. And no taxes to worry about unless you've got a real stiff conscience. Payable in cash every damned Friday as long as I'm open. Fair enough?"

The point has been made that Ernie Perkins was a damned good poker player. If this had not been the case, his mouth would have dropped open, his eyes would have stared woodenly, and he would have gaped in a markedly piscatorial fashion. This did not happen. As it was, a certain measure of surprise showed in his face. This was inevitable. When you're expecting an offer of a hundred dollars, a flat fee, and you get an offer of five thousand dollars a year instead, you are surprised.

"You thought it was a flat hundred," she said. "I'm not that stupid, chief. I don't want to give you small money. I want you to get a nice piece of change from my business. That way it'll stay open."

He nodded slowly. "Uh-huh," he said. "It makes sense."

"And the money covers more than staying open," she went on. "I want to be able to call for help if I run into trouble. I'm having a phone installed in the trailer. I want to have a cop come running if somebody makes trouble."

"That's easy enough."

"And no trouble from the sheriff," she said. "One payoff is enough. You can find a way to pay him and get rid of him in one lump sum. He won't cross you. Whereas he might back up on me."

He grinned automatically. The girl was smart. She knew how to gauge people, how to line up one against another and balance things off neatly. You had to give her credit.

And her proficiency pleased him. If somebody was going to run a whorehouse in Coldwater, it would be better if it was a smart one than a dumb one. It would be easier to cover for her, easier to look the other way when somebody got upset. He couldn't help feeling damned glad she was around.

"Is it a deal, chief?"

"It's a deal."

She opened her purse, took out an envelope. "Here's for this week," she said. "One hundred dollars, cash on the head of the barrel. The next payment comes Friday. I pay in advance. It makes the bookkeeping that much easier. You want me to drop it off here or you want to come around for it?"

He thought that one over. Either way would not be good, he knew. Either way too many people would make the connection. It just didn't look good when the police chief and the local madam were seen together all the time. It made a bad name for the chief. The town wouldn't like it.

"Let's see," he said. "You don't happen to have a messenger you could send down, do you? It'd make it a hell of a lot easier for the pair of us."

She thought for a moment, then smiled hugely. It would be the perfect job for Clay—running errands between a whore and a cop.

"Just some kid," Ernie Perkins went on. "Some kid who runs errands for you."

"I've got someone," she said, the smile still on her face. "He's not exactly a kid. But he'll do just fine."

BETTY TAYLOR WAS TALKING. Her husband was looking at her but he was not listening to a word she said. His mind was somewhere else entirely.

She's not a pretty woman, he thought. I love her and I enjoy living with her, but when you come right down to it she just plain isn't a pretty woman. She's a plain woman, really. Not that I ever minded her looks. Not that it matters too much what your wife looks like. A wife is for more than that. A wife is to talk to and to be with and to cook your meals and to bring up your children.

But she isn't a pretty woman.

"I'm going over to Thelma's," she was saying now, and this time be heard her. "A bunch of the girls are getting together. We'll play a little canasta, I guess."

"You women," he said automatically. "Canasta."

"With you it's poker," she said. "And with me it's canasta. Canasta's cheaper."

"You like it when I win, don't you?"

"I'm teasing," she said, grinning. She stood up, bent down to give him a quick kiss. "I'll be back by midnight," she said. "You'll be home?"

"Sure," he said. "Where am I going to go?"

WHERE *WAS* HE GOING to go?

That was a damn good question, Will thought. By all rules he was going to stay home, leaf through a magazine, maybe stare at the television for awhile. Because he certainly wasn't going to go to the trailer. The cathouse trailer.

No, he wouldn't go there.

Because what was waiting there for him? Nothing at all, naturally. Only a beautiful blonde with a shape like Marilyn Monroe. Only the most beautiful girl he'd ever laid eyes on, a girl named Marna who was heaven to look at and a delight to touch and pure pleasure between the sheets.

And she *liked* him. That was the part that was so god-awful hard to believe. But there was no reason for Clay Duncan to lie to him, not about something like that. Besides, he had the feeling all along that he was a little more to her than an ordinary cash customer. She had seemed to like him even then in the few minutes they were together.

Of course whores were always supposed to be like that, to listen to men talk about them. But he couldn't even think of Marna as a whore. What he and she did, it wasn't like going to a whore. It was nicer. They did it as though they were in love.

Maybe she was in love with him.

Hell, he thought. One roll in the hay with a ten-dollar trollop and she's in love with me. Twenty times a day she makes it and she's in love with me.

Sure.

But the thought kept intruding. Maybe it was because he wanted to *believe* it, he thought. It was silly—all it could do was louse up his marriage, and he didn't want to do that. He never should have gone to the trailer in the first place. It was a damn fool idea from the beginning.

But he couldn't help it. It wasn't just that Betty was no raving beauty. That was only part or it. Hell, it didn't make all that much difference what a woman looked like once the lights were out. That wasn't it.

It was more that Betty made love just about as well as she looked. She just plain didn't enjoy it, and there was no getting around it. She was willing, all right. She'd cooperate any time he wanted her to, never playing sick or tired the way some women did some of the time. It was more that she wasn't any good at it. She didn't get much of a kick out of it and she didn't know what to do once they got going. Willing or not, she just wasn't any good.

Marna was different.

Marna was entirely different, and when you added that to the way she looked you came up with trouble. Marna in a bed was a brand-new experience when you were used to a woman like Betty. Marna was warm as a Franklin stove, and you could tell that she wasn't just putting it on. She loved every minute or it and she knew just what to do.

It made a difference.

He lit a cigarette and dragged on it. You're just laying yourself wide open for trouble, he told himself. You're just taking your foot and shoving it half down your damn throat. You want to stay in your own yard and keep away from that yellow-haired gal. She's nothing but trouble.

But what trouble could it be?

Just once more, he thought. Just one more time and then he would forget all about her. Just once more, so that he wouldn't forget what it was like with a beautiful woman who knew what to do and who loved to do it.

He couldn't really afford it. Ten dollars was a lot of money when you were earning what he was earning. But he could manage. He'd cut down a little on cigarettes, and he'd tell Betty he lost more at the poker table than he had, and she would never find out about the extra ten-spot.

Well, why not?

He had the time. She'd be gone until close to midnight, and even if she came back while he was out he could always tell her he'd taken a run into town for cigarettes or something.

Just once he told himself. He had the time and he had the money, and the girl was there waiting for him. Just one last time, one last fling, so that he would know what it was like and never forget. Not that there was much chance of him forgetting someone like Marna anyway. But he wanted to make sure, wanted to try her once more and see if she was as good the second time around as she had been the first.

Maybe she wouldn't be. Maybe the second time would be no different from Betty. And that would be fine, he thought. That would cure him once and for all, and then he'd be set.

He checked his wallet—he had plenty of money. Then he opened the door of the trailer and stepped outside. Clay had said the trailer would be on the mill road a half-mile away. That was easy enough. He could walk there and nobody would even notice the car was gone.

He headed down a road, his arms swinging easily at his sides. He was filled with anticipation now. He could hardly wait.

Maybe she loved him. That would be one for the books, he thought. That would really be one for the books.

JAN AND MARNA WERE in the office. Lizzie was busy turning a trick. Andrea was in the washroom. Jan was looking out the window. She saw him coming, the long tall figure familiar now.

"That's him," she said.

"The one you meant?"

Jan nodded. "He's coming now," she said. "Be here in a minute or two. You got everything straight?"

"I think so."

There really wasn't a hell of a lot to get straight, Jan thought. But you had to be especially careful with a girl like Marna. The blonde wasn't exactly top-heavy with brains. Even when the instructions were disarmingly simple you had to repeat them at least three times.

And even then you weren't sure they'd soaked in. You had to check.

"Go over it," she said now. "He's coming here. What do you do when he gets here?"

Marna sighed. "I greet him like a long-lost brother," she said. "I recognize him by name. His name is Willie."

"Will."

"Will," Marna repeated. "Anyway, he picks me and we go to my room. But what if he doesn't pick me?"

"Don't worry about it."

Marna thought that one over. "We go to my room," she said. "And I throw my arms around him and tell him how I missed him and everything. I do it up brown. I make him think I'm in love with him, but really and truly."

Jan nodded. "Don't lay it on too thick," she said. "But make a real production out of it. Treat him special."

"Uh-huh. Then I give him a time he'll never forget. And then I take the ten dollars and I give it back to him. That's the part I don't get, Jan. Why give the money back?"

Jan sighed heavily. "I'll pay you the ten," she said. "Don't worry why."

"But why take it in the first place if I'm going to give it back again? I don't get it."

"Oh, Christ," she said. "You don't *have* to get it, stupe. You're supposed to be selling this dope a line about how much he sends you. Right?"

Marna nodded.

"So you take the money. Then you give it back and he thinks he must have been the world's greatest lover or you wouldn't have done it. See? Look, don't worry about the why part. Just follow orders. Good enough?"

"I guess so."

"Fine. Here he comes, sweetie. Be good to him."

The door opened and Will Taylor stepped into the room. He looked embarrassed, but then his eyes caught Marna's and something happened to him. All at once there was a smile on his face and a lump in his throat. Jan noted both with approval.

And Marna played the scene well. She was magnificent. She called out his name, and she hurried to him, and she took one of his hands in both of hers and looked straight into his eyes. She told him just how glad she was to see him, and how she was hoping he would come back, and she was perfect in the role.

Then she stopped short, pretending that she was embarrassed to give herself away in front of Jan. That was the clincher. Jan wanted to break out into applause at that point but managed to contain herself until the two of them were out of the office and into the blonde's room.

Then she started to giggle.

It would be easy now. When the hick got his ten-spot handed to him he would be sunk fifty fathoms under water. He wouldn't have a chance.

Poor Will Taylor, she thought. And poor Betty Taylor. And how nice it was to see them both get it in the neck.

Pretty soon it would be poor Lily Sue and Poor Jack. And then, by God, she wouldn't just giggle.

She'd laugh like hell.

Chapter 5

WHEN LIZZIE JACKSON WENT to town, she didn't walk down Water Street. She knew better. She was a Negro, and consequently she walked on River Road.

Now there was no rule to this effect, of course. Kentucky is not the Deep South, for one thing, and its racial rules were not formalized by any means. But Lizzie knew intuitively that fewer heads would turn and fewer mouths would mumble unpleasantness to themselves if she walked through the Negro section of Coldwater than if she came promenading down the main street of the town. River Road was a Coldwater approximation of Lenox Avenue, coming about as close to the original as Waler Street did to Broadway. Lizzie didn't exactly feel at home there, but she knew that, in the eyes of the town, it was where she was supposed to be.

While River Road was not precisely a slum, there was an obvious economic disparity between it and Water Street. Water Street was hardly Fifth Avenue, just as it was hardly Broadway, but the buildings themselves were in infinitely better shape and the stores carried a slightly better quality of merchandise. River Road was more residential, since few

shops were strictly for Negroes in a city the size of Coldwater. There was a barber shop, of course, and a restaurant, and
a trio of taverns. There was a lunch counter and a small pool
hall. There were lower-class shops that catered more to the
Negro trade than to whites.

A long street of dull gray clapboard buildings. Brown
faces everywhere. River Road.

And here we are, Lizzie thought. A million miles from
125th Street and we know just where to go and what to do.
A million miles from anywhere and we know to wait for the
Man, and where to find him, and what he'll be like.

Instinct, she thought. Like a homing pigeon. You had
to know just where to go and what to do, and it was born
into you the minute you stuck your head out of the womb
and came up brown instead of white. There were things you
had to know if you were a Negro in America. There were
survival mechanisms. There was an inborn in-groupishness
you couldn't afford to lose.

It wasn't hipness, because the spades in Coldwater could
hardly be accused of being hip. They were a little closer to
being with it than the Coldwater ofays, but that was saying
little indeed. They listened to rock 'n' roll instead of hard
bop, and they ate pone and chitterlings like field hands,
and if you dropped them in the middle of Harlem they'd be
thoroughly terrified.

But they were still spades, and it made a difference. It
gave you an automatic in, a sense of belonging that didn't

dissipate itself no matter how different you felt yourself to be. Pigment was more than skin deep. It had to be, or you couldn't keep swinging.

And you had to keep swinging, she thought. Because the little brown cigarettes were all gone, and even a town like Coldwater had to have The Man, the dream man who had more little brown cigarettes if the price was right. She hadn't needed a man in New York. Her own little sweet man took care of all that. He took every penny she made, and in return for that he paid her rent and bought her clothes every once in a while and kept her supplied with a dollar's worth of tea a day. She had figured it out once—he spent maybe five dollars a day on her, and when the day came that she turned over less than ninety dollars to him she got a beating.

A cool arrangement. A lovely arrangement, but not for her. She had herself a sweet man, a pimp, and he had himself the cushiest living in the world. But what else could you do? A girl had to have somebody. A girl couldn't swing her rear around all by herself or she died of loneliness. And on top of that an Uptown girl without a man leading her was an outlaw broad, a lone wolf chick that nobody wanted to see around.

So you got your sweet man and you paid him your money. And that was one good thing about Coldwater. She kept that bread for herself. She salted it away, and when she went back to the Apple she'd have a big stack of chips, enough to set herself up in something clean and cool and nice.

Maybe.

But she missed him. That was the lousy thing about it, she missed him.

Damn.

And double-damn.

Damn it to hell and back.

You could put out for the world and it didn't make a thing. If you had somebody of your own you were set, it was all right, you could move around a bit. But without that pimp, without that sweet man, you were swinging by yourself.

It was tough.

She broke off her train of thought when she came to the bar. It was a hole in the wall named Blue Moon, and at that hour of the day, late in the afternoon, it was almost empty. Lizzie walked into it. A few heads turned to look at her, to get a good look at the colored hooker who was working in the chick's cathouse. Eyes studied her, then ignored her. She went to the bar and ordered whiskey and water from the fat bartender. She paid for her drink and carried it to a table along the far wall. She tossed off the shot without tasting it, and she waited for something to happen.

It took half an hour.

Then she heard the voice. Close to her, next to her, was The Man. His voice was not a Harlem voice. It was southern, but it had the confidence and authority that could only belong to The Man.

"Hello, brown gal," The Man said. "You got room for company?"

She looked up and saw a very thin light-skinned Negro standing at the table. He wore tight grey slacks, a grey shirt buttoned at the neck, a dark grey sport jacket. His shoes were yellow deerskin. The style had been extremely popular in Harlem circles three or four years back.

"Sit," she said.

He sat down. He was holding a bottle of Cincinnati beer in one hand and a glass in the other. She watched as he tilted the glass and poured beer into it very slowly and elaborately.

He did not get any head on the beer. He took a small, precise sip of the beer and set the glass on the table top. He set the glass down three times to make three interlocking rings of moisture, then moved the glass aside.

"Ballantine," he said. "See the rings?"

She nodded.

"You got a name?" The Man asked.

She told him her name.

"Mine is Royal," The Man said. "Royal Peters."

She nodded again.

"The way I hear," Royal said, "you sell something. Right?"

Her eyes widened slightly. He couldn't be a customer. That didn't make much sense. "I sell something," she said. "But I'm not selling right now."

"That's what I thought," he said. "I figured you might be buying. I sell something myself. You might call me a man of business. Nice New York type of phrase."

She hadn't made a mistake. He was pushing. Which was fine with her.

"We can talk here," Royal Peters said. "We talk quiet and nobody minds. What you want to buy, Lizzie girl?"

She studied his face. He had a thin moustache like a pencil-line. His eyes were sharp, intent, and they never lost their sharpness even when he was talking lazily and taking his small sips of beer.

"Tea," she said.

His narrow eyebrows went up a notch. "Fooled me," he said. "Always thought you big-town gals were too grown up for Mary Jane. Thought you used hard stuff."

"Is that all you sell?"

He chuckled softly. "Oh, no," he said. "No, I can sell you what you want, Lizzie. Nice-sized bombers at fifty cents a shot. No catnip in it and no Bull Durham. Good stuff."

The price was around half the New York tariff. "How far do you cut it?"

"Not cut at all. Straight goods. Fair enough?"

"Fair enough," she said.

His lips curled in a smile. "You have eyes right now? You like to go for a flying trip?"

Why not? She had a few hours before it was time for work. And it had been a while since the last of the five sticks from New York had wafted her up and away.

"I could make it," she said.

"Seeing as you're a new customer, I've got a large idea."

She waited.

"We go to my house," he said. "Just a little shack a ways away. And we boot it around together. No charge, seeing as you're a new customer. We both take off and fly."

The bait was transparent and the fish hook was plainly visible inside it. Sure, the pot would be free. And so would the love that came after it. They'd swing together, and then they'd make it together at his pad.

And then the pitch would come. Not right away, maybe, but it would be there soon enough. *You need a manager, girl. Somebody to take good care of you. You making a lot of money, girl. You don't watch out somebody takes it all away from you. You ought to turn it over to Royal for safekeeping. Royal can take good care of you. Besides, Royal loves you, girl.*

The old routine. And it would start, sure as anything, would start the minute she nodded her head and agreed that it would be a kick to turn on together. He was a funny little stud and they would have laughed at him in Harlem, but they weren't in Harlem now and he was smooth as silk by Coldwater standards.

And he was the only man around.

The thing to do was keep it strictly business, she thought. Insist on paying cash for the sticks and keep your distance the rest of the time. No free trips to the moon, and no rolls, and no sweet man. Because a sweet man wasn't so sweet at all. He was sour as battery acid and twice as likely to etch into you, twice as apt to burn you.

But—

But it would be so nice to be with him. To be with a guy who wasn't paying you, to be with a sweet coffee-colored man who treated you like a woman and loved you like a woman and made you feel like a woman. So nice. So very nice, and it would be only this one time and that would be all. She wouldn't wind up on his string, wouldn't wind up with a pimp taking all her money. She'd be careful.

And one time wouldn't hurt. Just one time, so that she felt a little better inside, so that pot and sex could go together like a horse and carriage, like love and marriage, like everything that went well together.

Just once.

Once wouldn't hurt.

So she smiled, a smile that was only partially a phony, and she stood up from the table.

"That sounds nice," she said. "Let's go."

JAN WAS EXPECTING A visitor.

The stage was set for a visitor. And the invitation had been extended. The girls were gone—Andy and Marna had been dispatched to a movie in another town down the road, with strict instructions not to return until after dinner. Lizzie was in town and would probably remain there until about the same time that the girls returned.

So Jan was alone.

She passed the time while she waited by going over her account ledger, checking the income and the expenditures and seeing how she was doing financially. She was doing very well, all things taken into account. The hundred a week which was paid every Friday by Clay to Ernie Perkins hardly made a dent in her bankroll. Even with the generous eighty percent which she permitted the girls to retain, her twenty percent plus her own earnings added up to a considerable sum.

She was doing fine.

But there was one thing more which had to be done, and when her visitor arrived she would be able to attend to it. Her visitor was the one person she really wanted to see. Her visitor meant a good deal more to her than the net receipts. Those were simply entries of profit, simply chips in the pot that told her how well she was doing from a business standpoint. But business had not been the main objective of the operation from the beginning, so the profits of the place were only a small indication of her success.

She lit a cigarette and smoked it in silence.

She waited.

Then there was a knock on the door of the trailer, a soft and discreet knock. She called for the knocker to come inside, and with elaborate casualness she turned around in her chair and looked at the person she had been waiting to see.

Jack Appleton.

He stood in the doorway, his frame filling it, and she looked him up and down slowly and felt the hate returning, filling her as full as he filled the doorjamb. This was the visitor. This was the man she had to get even with, the man who had ditched her, the reason for her return to Coldwater.

She masked her hatred. She actually smiled a smile which he did not return, and while her insides churned with loathing she told him to come inside, to close the door.

He came in.

"It's about time you dropped by," she said breezily.

"It is?"

"I've missed you," she said. "My own ex-husband doesn't even give me a welcome home when I come back to town. It's a hell of a note."

He didn't say anything.

"I thought you'd drop around. After all, you're to thank for what I am today. I mean, you taught me everything I know, Jack. Now I'm cashing in on it. You deserve a certain amount of credit. I'm making a lot of money, Jack. If I keep on this way I'll be as rich as your father-in-law. Won't that be something? Your ex-wife as rich as your father-in-law?"

He still didn't say anything. She tried to read his face and failed. He was mad at her; it wasn't hard to tell that much. But that was all she could see.

"It must be a switch for you," she said. "Being married to money, I mean. Remember the way we used to scrape by on your pay? No more of that for you, lucky boy."

"We live on my salary."

She laughed. "Sure you do," she said. "Old Brad Finch never slips his daughter a penny, does he?"

He didn't answer her.

"Well, you got what you wanted. And so did I. A nice tidy cathouse that brings in plenty of money. Who could ask for anything more than that? We both came out of it nicely, Jack."

He stood with his hands on his hips. "Your pimp said you wanted to see me," he said.

"You mean Clay?" She laughed. "He's not a pimp, honey. He's an errand boy."

He ignored the correction. "He said you wanted to talk to me. He said I might be able to get you to leave town."

"Is that what Clay said?"

He nodded.

"Silly thing for him to say," she said. "Why would you want me to leave town? I'm certainly not getting in your way. But I'm glad to see you, Jack. For old time's sake. I've been hoping you'd drop by and spend some time with me. I get lonely, you know. I get awfully lonely."

His temper flared. "Lonely? That's not the way I hear it. I hear you get taken twenty times a night."

"Sometimes more than that," she said. "On a good night."

"So that makes you lonely?"

"Lonely for you," she purred. "I'd kind of like you right

now, Jack. You're the best I ever had, baby. The best ever. I wouldn't even charge you, Jack."

"I've got better at home, Jan."

Her laughter was harsh. "You think so? You think she's so damn good? She may have plenty of tramp in her, but that doesn't make any difference. I know tricks she never heard of, Jack. You remember some of the tricks I know. I've learned others, too. You learn a lot in this business."

"Jan—"

She cupped a breast in each hand. She was wearing no bra beneath her flimsy blouse and the breasts were warm through the thin material. She held them like an offering.

"These are nicer than hers," she said.

His eyes were dark. "I better go," he said.

But she moved quickly, stepping around him to block the doorway and prevent him from getting out. "You stay awhile," she said. "You stay. Momma won't bite you. Not unless you want me to, that is. And I don't have to bite, either. I can do nice things, Jack."

"Damn it—"

"Relax now," she said. "You came over here for a reason, and there's no sense in you leaving without getting something accomplished. You want to get me out of town, don't you?"

"Naturally."

She looked up at him innocently. "Why, Jack? Why try to get rid of me? I'm not doing you any harm."

"You're ruining the whole damn camp," he said. "You've got some wives walking around jealous for no good reason at all. You've got other husbands cheating on their wives and spending money they can't afford to lose. You've got poor Will Taylor walking around with stars in his eyes. Everybody but his wife knows what's going on between him and that blonde whore of yours. She's so much in love with him that she can't see it. And he used to be in love with her the same way until your blonde got into the act."

"That happens sometimes," she said sweetly. "Sometimes a pretty girl can steal another woman's husband. It happened to me once. I could tell you about it, Jack."

He ignored the dig. "You're ruining everybody's morale. I wouldn't give a damn if there was an ordinary house around. They're good for the single men, give 'em an outlet they need. But you've got something different going. I don't like it."

"Is that the only reason, Jack?"

He looked at her.

"I think you're afraid," she went on. "I think you're afraid because you can't help wanting to get a crack at me again. Isn't that more like it?"

"You're crazy, Jan."

"I don't think so," she said. "I think I'm right for a change. I think you're scared stiff."

He shook his head angrily. He was about to say something but she didn't give him a chance.

"Tell me the truth," she said. "Take a good look at me. Boobs and hips and everything else. And then tell me you don't have the lightest desire to make love with me."

His eyes made their way from her face to her feet and back again. "No desire," he said. "I don't even want to look at you. You make me sick to my stomach."

She laughed in his face. "We had too much, Jack. We had a lot going for us. Oh, we were mismatched in a lot of respects. But we were pretty phenomenal when the lights were out. And don't tell me you can't remember how good it was. You couldn't possibly forget it in a million years."

"You can get tired of plain sex, Jan."

"But it takes time. You can get tired of a little minx like Lily Sue, too. Lily Sue Finch. But it's Appleton now, isn't it? Lily Sue Appleton. Sounds sweet as sugar."

He didn't answer her.

"Kiss me, Jack."

"Get out of my way!"

She laughed again, leaning her weight against him. "Okay," she said. "You don't want me at all. We had something but it's gone forever. That's fine, Jack. That ought to make it just that much easier for you."

"To do what?"

"To get rid of me," she said. "To get me out of Coldwater for keeps. It'll be a cinch."

"What are you driving at?"

"It's simple," she said. "All you have to do is make love

to me. Just once. Then I'll pack up and get out of your life forever. If you still want me to."

He stared at her. "You must be out of your mind."

"Why? It's a good deal for you, Jack. I don't mean a thing to you. So you could make love to me without feeling a thing. It would be like being a machine for a few minutes. And your wife would never know about it."

"You'd tell her."

"I could tell her anyway. She wouldn't believe me any more just because it was true."

He shook his head. "You're nuts," he said. "You're just plain nuts. Now get the hell out of my way. I'm leaving."

She reached out, took hold of him. "Maybe you'll change your mind," she said. "This used to belong to me."

He slapped her hand away. Then, when she reached for him again, his fist exploded against the side of her jaw. The pain was a searing knife through the side of her head. The world went slowly from grey to black and she slumped to the floor, losing consciousness for several minutes.

When she came out of it, slowly and painfully, he was gone. She went to the sink and washed, pressing a cold cloth against the side of her jaw. The swelling went down but the pain remained relatively constant.

Well, he was going to pay for it. Nobody got away with taking a punch at her. Right now he must be feeling pretty pleased with himself, she thought. Turned down her proposition and knocked her flat in the bargain. Well, let him have his fun. Pretty soon the shoe would be on the other foot. And then she'd use it to kick his teeth down his throat.

"WHAT YOU'VE GOT TO watch out for," Clay Duncan said, "is that Lily Sue broad. She's a spitfire, that one. And it's not her so much. It's her old man."

"Brad Finch?"

"That's the one," he said. He stirred his coffee with a spoon. "He's a powerhouse, honey. And he'll do anything his sweet little daughter wants him to do."

It was late at night. Two days had passed since Jan had confronted Jack Appleton. Now the trailer was parked again on its plot at the trailer camp. The night had been a profitable one. Now she and Clay were drinking coffee in the office while the other girls slept. The sky was already lightening. It was grey outside, the hour before the dawn, but she was not tired yet.

"I've got the fix in with Ernie," she said. "Won't that stop Finch?"

"Finch?" He laughed unhappily. "He's a hell of a strong man in this town. Strong in this part of the state. He could buy Ernie and sell him a few times over. And Ernie has to listen to him. If Brad puts the pressure on, I think you'll be in trouble."

She digested that. "Then we pin Finch down," she said. "I can't stand the old bastard anyway. I'd get a kick out of nailing his skin to the nearest wall."

"What did he do to you?"

"He arranged the divorce. Instead of taking his under-age brat out to the woodshed and waling the tar out of her when she told him she was sleeping with a married man, he went out with his checkbook in his hand and bought the married man for her for a husband. That's what he did."

Clay nodded. He picked up his coffee cup and sipped the coffee. "And what are you going to do to him?"

She thought about it. "Get one of the girls after him," she said. "Take a picture or two of him in bed with one of the girls. That ought to do it."

"With Finch? He'd laugh in your face."

"I could use Lizzie," she suggested. "It might not do Brad Finch any good to have a picture of him and a colored girl floating around town."

He shook his head wearily. "No difference in the world," he said, "Finch would laugh it off and run you out of town. He's got a big reputation as a chaser. Except that he doesn't have to chase too hard, not with his money. You couldn't get any place with him."

"I'll find a way," she said. "No man is invulnerable. If you pry a little bit you get a stranglehold on any man who was ever born. I don't have anything to worry about."

They lapsed into silence. Jan stared moodily into her cup of coffee, then glanced across the table at Clay. He was looking out the window at the morning.

"I got a better idea," he said slowly.

"Let's hear it."

"You could junk the whole thing," he said. "You could get out of town while you've got nothing to worry about."

"Just like that?"

"Just like that."

"You're off your rocker," she said. "Why should I quit while I'm ahead?"

"Because it's better than waiting until you're behind," he told her. "And because you could do better things than waste your time running a whorehouse on wheels."

"Look who got religion," she said. "If I go, who's going to take care of the business? You?"

"To hell with the business," he said. "And no, I won't be taking over. I'll be going with you."

"What?"

"You heard me right," he said. "It makes a hell of a lot more sense to me, Jan. I'm crazy about you, whether you know it or not. I don't want to share you with the world. And I don't want to see you get shoved around by this rotten town. I want you all to myself for good."

"Well, I'll be damned. Hey, you're forgetting something, aren't you? It seems to me you've still got a wife. Or are you forgetting all about her?"

"I ought to," he said. "She forgot all about me. But that's no problem. I can get a divorce from her in a week."

"And then what?"

"Then we can be married."

It was hard for her to hold back her laughter. Marry him? Why in hell would she want to marry him, for God's sake? It was getting ridiculous.

"Hang on," she said. "Hang on a minute. Let's take this from the top, huh? What's all this about marrying me. This is a new one, Clay."

"It's what I want."

"Really?"

"Really."

"How come?"

He drew a breath. "Because I'm in love with you," he said. "That's all. I can't explain it and I don't want to try. I'm in love with you. I don't want to be but I can't help it."

"Are you sure you're not confusing love? That happens, you know."

"I know it happens, Jan. And I've had enough to tell the difference. I love you. I want to marry you. And that's all I can say about it."

It was plenty, she thought sardonically. It was a pretty earthshaking announcement, all things considered, and she wasn't sure quite what to make of it. She couldn't imagine why in hell he thought he was in love with her but it didn't seem to be the time to argue with him. If he wanted to think so, fine. That was his business. As far as marriage went, she would hate to sit on a hot stove until she married the clod. But for the time being he could think whatever he wanted. It wouldn't hurt.

"I'll tell you what," she said. "Why don't we change the subject?"

"To what?"

"To bed," she said. "We haven't been to bed in a while, Clay. And I'm in the mood."

"Now?"

"No time like the present, is there?"

He thought about it. "Are you sure you feel like it, Jan?"

Now that was a new one. Since when did he give a damn whether she felt like it or not? All he ever cared about was whether or not she was willing, and her own desires never had much to do with it. Maybe this was part of the love kick he was on.

She decided that the best thing to do with him was get him into a bedroom as quickly as possible. He'd been a good boy and he deserved a reward. Besides, she actually felt in the mood, as it happened. The kind of thing she and Clay did was not something she habitually got much kick out of. But this evening she had an idea she was going to enjoy it.

Not this evening, she thought. Not evening at all. Morning, really. A grey morning, and time to go to bed.

"I'm sure," she said. "Come on, lover. Come to Mama. Mama's hungry."

They laughed together. Then he stood up and took her in his arms, his mouth hungry for hers. She returned his kiss with passion that she did not have to feign, edging her tongue into his mouth, drilling holes in his chest with her breasts, pressing her body against his.

"The bedroom," she said, her voice oddly husky.

"What's the matter with right here?"

"Come on, dammit. I can't wait."

They left the office and went to Jan's room. She turned and closed the door. They kissed again and this time his hand closed around her breast and squeezed firmly but gently.

"Nice," he muttered.

"You think so?"

"I know so."

She giggled. She moved away from him and pulled her dress clear over her head in one movement, tossing it to a chair. She was wearing nothing at all under it.

"If you like me so much," she said, "go ahead and play with me. I like it."

They sat on the bed and he caressed her using hands and lips.

"All right," she said finally. "Now I show you how nice the world is."

He stretched out on her bed, his face relaxed into a smile, his eyes closed.

And she went to work. It went on for some time.

Then it was time for the finale, time for the end of the game. Again she kissed him and again she caressed him.

"Jan—"

She looked up, looked at his face. He was sitting upright, his lips trembling with passion. "Jan, you don't have to do that. It isn't right to make you do that."

Was he flipping his lid?

"I love you," he said. "I don't want you to do anything you don't want to do. I mean it, Jan!"

She sighed. "Lie down," she said.

"Jan—"

"I want to, stupid. Lie down."

Afterward, they slept for hours in each other's arms.

Chapter 6

IT WAS A STRANGE time for Will Taylor. There were days when he felt as though his life for the past few weeks was not a life at all but a weird and elusive dream, following a dream's patterns of illogic and disjointedness with little or no relationship to what he thought of as reality. There were nights when he sat over dinner with Betty, then made hectic and madcap love to Marna, and finally wound up lying awake in his own bed next to the dormant body of his wife once more. He would lie awake, staring at the darkness, and he would examine the schizoid state of his own emotions and the inexplicable patterns of his own behavior. Then he would become convinced that he was mad, or that the world was mad, or that everything was, quite simply, a dream.

But the dream never ended when morning came. Sometimes it was dispelled for a time, sometimes he awoke without thinking of Marna, but later in the day the hunger would return stronger than ever before and the dream, such as it was, would still be upon him.

What amazed him, more perhaps than anything else, was his own frightening ability to deceive, his talent for turning emotions on and off like a faucet. He could sit with

Betty, his desire for Marna, and he could discuss the weather or the day at camp or, in fact, almost anything. He could be calm and cool and collected, interested on the surface in everything Betty had to say, solicitous for her health and welfare.

And, hours later, he would be with Marna. And then all the wraps were off, all eyes open, and the two of them made love with a breathless zest that was completely overpowering. At those times, the world was gone and the dream turned undeniably to some wonderful abstract of Truth. When you were making love to a woman like Marna (if there were any other woman in the world like her, which he doubted) somehow there was no room left in your mind for outside thoughts. The act itself was too all-embracing, too monumental to be disturbed by nagging guilt or split allegiances.

She never charged him money for her favors, not since the one time at the beginning. Since then, it had been free, every time, and when he had tried to pay her she had turned him down hard.

"It has to be free," she told him. "Because I want it as much as you do. I won't even let you give me presents. I don't want presents from you. Can't you understand?"

He could understand well enough. Understanding was one thing; believing the depth of his good fortune was another. But she made him believe her, and he had her almost nightly and paid nothing.

Eventually, he knew, things were going to come to a head. They couldn't go on this way forever. Even if he was determined to go on leading a double life, he wouldn't be able to do so indefinitely. Marna would want him on a full-time basis, or Betty would find out about his infidelity and raise hell, or something.

And he knew that he wouldn't want it to go on this way much longer. Sooner or later he was going to have to make a choice between the two of them, between Betty and Marna. It was going to be a pretty messy choice, and that was why he was putting it off as long as he could. Betty was the perfect wife, kind and thoughtful and breathtakingly efficient, the perfect helpmate and soulmate. And Marna was the perfect mistress, a sweet female all the time and an absolute delight when the lights were out.

He thought about science fiction movies he had seen, where a scientist discovers a ray that turns people inside-out and similar nonsense. If only he could take the two of them and make one woman out of them. Or if only he could turn the clock back to the days when a man had a wife to bear his children and look after his house and a mistress to keep his bed warm.

It was a problem.

But, in the meantime, he made the most of it. He took his pleasure with Marna and stayed married to Betty and waited for the world to fall in.

ANDREA DIDN'T LIKE THE whole thing.

She rolled over onto her side and reached for the pack of cigarettes on the bedside table. She was tired, but she knew better than to try to sleep. Sleep was a long ways off. Even after a hard night's work, even after the moaning and grunting of all the men who had taken incomplete possession of her body that evening, sleep remained out of the question for the time being. She put a cigarette between her lips, scratched a match and lit it. The match bathed the trailer compartment with a shallow yellow glow. She held the match between thumb and forefinger and looked at the girl in bed beside her.

She was sleeping like a log. Sure, she thought. Little Marna doesn't have to toss and turn. Little Marna's snug in the arms of Morpheus.

Damn her!

Not tonight, Andy. Not tonight. I just don't feel like it tonight. Tomorrow, okay?

It was always tomorrow. And, on those relatively rare occasions when the blowsy blonde decided that, by God, she *did* feel like it for a change, it just wasn't the same. It was almost as though Andy herself was a man and Marna was turning a trick with her mind and soul turned off in the process. She remembered the time when she had gotten so sick and disgusted with the whole thing that, when it was over, she had gotten up, dressed, and had left a crisp ten-dollar bill on the table.

That had been nasty, and it had hurt Marna terribly, and there had been a terrible tearful scene during which the two of them cried a great deal and wound up making love that satisfied them both.

But since then it had just gotten worse.

Andy knew why. Hell, she was no dummy. When the girl you're in love with suddenly cools down, you look around to see who else is interesting her. And you think of the man who's making it for free—Jan's bright idea, damn her to hell—and you make a little connection between this guy and her attitude toward you. You have to have junk for brains to miss the connection. It's not that subtle.

So Andy was mad.

She took a deep drag on the cigarette and watched the red tip glow. It was dark in the room and she couldn't see the cloud of smoke when she exhaled it. She remembered hearing somewhere that half the pleasure was gone when you couldn't see the smoke, that you enjoyed the act of smoking a good deal less as a result. She tried it again with another drag, drawing it way down into her lungs, then blowing it out. As far as she could tell, it didn't make a damn bit of difference whether you saw the smoke or not.

This didn't make her any less angry.

Angry at Jan, for setting up the stupid bit where Marna slept with Taylor for free. If Jan wanted to bust up Taylor's marriage, that was fine and dandy. But why the hell did she have to bust up the thing she and Marna had going?

So she was mad at Jan. She was also mad at Taylor, naturally. He was her rival, in a strange and ludicrous way that would have been worth a laugh if it hadn't been so mind-freezing. She would have cheerfully strangled him. But what kind of rival was he? In one sense he was Marna's patsy, a guy she was carrying along for the ride. In another sense he was taking Andy's own place in the blonde girl's love life. It was nutty.

And, ultimately, she was mad at Marna. That was the hardest part. It is no thing of overwhelming joy to be mad as hell at a girl with whom you are simultaneously in love. It is nerve-wracking.

Damn it!

And what could she do about it? Not a hell of a lot, when you came right down to it. She could run out on Marna, but what would that get her? It would be a clear-cut case of lopping off her boobs to spite her chest.

The trouble lay in the fact that she needed Marna more than she ought to need anyone. Previously this didn't hurt, since it was balanced by a comparable need on Marna's part. Now, however, things were changed. And she was up the creek in a lead canoe without a paddle, and the lead canoe had sprung a leak.

It would have been different in New York. There she would have had no problems in getting rid of any ache that jealousy caused. Once or twice she had grown jealous in New York, generally for no good reason, and each time it happened she solved it simply and expediently. She merely got out of the apartment and found herself a pick-up. This was easy, since New York was swimming in lesbians. All she had to do was hie herself down to Club Shady Lane or The Abattoir and find a properly edible young thing who had nothing on for the night. Then they'd make a quick trip to a convenient room and all Andrea's troubles would vanish like smoke.

Speaking of which, she took a final drag on her cigarette and butted it in an ashtray. She sighed.

The remedy wouldn't work in Coldwater. There was an exciting total of two lesbians in the town, and she was one of them while Marna was the other, and this made things a little more than difficult. It made them impossible.

Damn it to hell!

She turned to look at Marna again, which was a mistake. She saw the soft warm curves of Marna. She saw the red slash of Marna's mouth and ached to kiss and be kissed by that mouth, to hold the big blonde close in her arms, to—

Men had it easy, she thought angrily. A man could go to a house when he needed a woman. But what could a girl do when *she* needed a woman? Not much of anything, she answered herself. Just lie and ache.

That Taylor. That rotten two-timing bastard. She wanted to settle with him, wanted to teach him a lesson.

But Taylor was the symptom, not the cause. There

wasn't really anything to do, and she was stuck in her lead canoe while the water poured in at her.

It was a mess.

IT WAS A MESS.

Jack Appleton lay in bed next to his wife and thought what a mess it really was. It had been a bad enough mess the day he had lost his temper and belted Jan on the snoot. Not that she hadn't deserved it. Jan deserved anything that happened to her. If somebody slit her throat with a rusty razor and did it so slow she died of tetanus instead of loss of blood, she deserved it.

But he was pretty sure it had been a mistake to belt her. It seemed to work the same way in human relationships as it did in the army, or in an athletic contest. A boxer who hated his opponent and gave way to his hate found himself on the canvas. A soldier who charged pillboxes in utter rage wound up being buried in several different pieces. It was okay to get mad, but you couldn't let the world know it.

That's right, he thought. Get all wrapped up in big thoughts while the walls fall in. But it seemed to make a certain amount of sense. Maybe there was no connection, but he had the feeling that the punch to the side of the jaw marked a turning-point in the already rotten conditions around the camp. They had been bad enough, and then they had taken a turn for the worse.

First of all, there was Will Taylor. According to most of

the guys, it was even money that Will was going to divorce Betty and take up with that blonde whore of his. It was also even money that mild, easy going Betty would, when she inevitably found out about the blazing affair between her husband and New York's answer to Madame de Pompadour, pick up gun or knife and kill (a) Will, (b) Marna, or (c) herself, or any two of them, or all three.

Then there was the town. It looked as though Jan had managed to get through to Chief Perkins, because any complaints that went to him, and there were plenty of them, seemed to roll off him like water off a mallard's topside. Complaints directed at the county sheriff fared about the same. Even when some public-spirited citizen tipped off the sheriff or chief as to the precise location on any particular evening, no raid was made, no man dispatched, and no results gained.

In fact, when one bozo from the base got drunk and started a mild-mannered melee going at the trailer, a cop appeared in no time at all. But he didn't close down the house or make arrests—nothing like that. He just plain knocked the living hell out of the poor drunk, using his nightstick as freely as any cop interrogating a cop killer, and he couldn't have looked more like Jan's personal bouncer if he'd tried.

This didn't make the town too happy, naturally enough. When your police chief is running interference for a madam, and when the madam isn't even a local girl-makes-bad to begin with, you don't exactly jump into the stratosphere and click your heels together and holler whoopee. And when the madam is sort of a gift from a trailer camp, sort of an Army Wife reject, and when you didn't like the army too much to begin with, thinking of them as oversexed, overpaid and over here, this doesn't exactly make you tell yourself over and over again that all men are brothers, especially soldiers.

There had been a few incidents, if you wanted to call them that. A single soldier at a rock 'n' roll hop had been coaxed outside by a jailbait type, at which signal three townies in specially imported black leather jackets had proceeded to kick the life out of him. Since the stomping boots hadn't arrived, their effectiveness had been limited. But three broken ribs was enough of a reward for the soldier, and he didn't get a Purple Heart in the bargain, just a warning from the base.

A window in one of the trailers was broken, probably by a rock, probably thrown by a townsman. What was remarkable, and what Jack could never quite understand, was why the good people of Coldwater vented their rage not upon Jan and the girls, who had caused the whole thing to begin with, but upon the base and the trailer camp, who were relatively innocent victims of the same disease. Hell, the townies even patronized the damn cathouse, when they were sufficiently affluent to be able to afford ten dollars.

It was a hell of a note.

It was especially annoying to Jack because he had been

thinking of himself as a sort of cornerstone of town-camp relations. He'd made the breech, sort of, by marrying a girl who was not only a townie but the daughter of the town's most solid citizen. Instead of him solidifying relations, though, the trailer was fixing things so that his own relations with his father-in-law were rapidly deteriorating. After all, Jan was the woman from whom Bradwell Finch had bought Jack his freedom. And, illogically enough, Brad considered him personally responsible for Jan's presence in Coldwater.

Which messed everything up. Messed it to the point that when Lily Sue asked her father to roll the trailer out of town once and for all, Finch had refused. "Let your husband get rid of 'em," he said. "He brought the bitch here in the first place. I paid her off once already. Let him toss her out of town."

Which was easier said than done.

Because it was very easy to say.

And impossible to do.

He rolled over and looked at Lily Sue, saw how peaceful she slept, how lovely she looked. He wondered what the whole mess was doing to her, how she was taking it. She hadn't said much about the trailer lately, and Lily Sue had never been one to internalize her feelings. When something was on her mind she didn't see any reason to keep it to herself. She would talk about damn near anything, and when she kept still it was because she had nothing important to talk about.

Now she seemed different. More distant, sort of. He wondered why this was so, and if it was a sign of anything in particular, any worry that was troubling her mind.

Damn Jan, he thought. Damn her a thousand times over. Damn her to hell and back.

She was trying to bust up his marriage. That much was obvious; she wasn't even trying to hide the fact. She was trying to worm her way between him and Lily Sue, just as she was trying to louse up Will and Betty Taylor, just as she was making things rough for every married couple in the camp.

But especially for him. She was getting even—or at least that was the way she looked at it. He was personally convinced most of the time that there wasn't a damned thing she could do, that the relationship between him and Lily Sue was firm enough and strong enough and well-rooted enough that nothing like Jan could knock it around. But there were times when he wasn't quite so sure of this, times when Jan looked awfully strong and he and Lily seemed to be relatively weak in comparison.

Of course there was one way to get her out of the place—or at least she said there was. A simple way, the way she talked about it. All he had to do was take her to bed.

That was all.

Just love her out of town.

Nice bait on her part. A cute move, and one that would ruin everything. One that would dynamite the whole routine, so that everything blew up in his face.

But why?

He thought about it for a moment, saw it suddenly in a way it had not occurred to him before. Actually, when you stopped to give it some thought, there was nothing wrong with it. The idea of sleeping once with Jan to get her out of town, that is. As she had said, if it didn't mean a thing to him it wouldn't hurt him one way or the other. It would be automatic and mechanical, a means to an end with no more meaning than that. Like taking a laxative.

Then why was he afraid of it? He'd slept with girls before without particularly wanting them, and he was sufficiently confident in the ability of his body to respond in proper fashion to the proper set of stimuli. And there was no apparent way for Lily Sue to find out—Jan could tell her it had happened just as effectively whether it was the truth or not.

So what was he afraid of?

The answer came back at him and he winced. He must be afraid he would enjoy it, afraid his ex-wife would have something that his present wife lacked. It made no sense— Lily Sue was the perfect wife, and he was missing nothing. So why worry about Jan's possible superiority when he knew better? He'd tried Jan before—hell, he'd been married to her long enough and he knew what she was like.

Why worry?

He decided that there might be something he hadn't thought of yet, something that would make the difference.

He still felt intuitively certain that sleeping with Jan would be the worst possible move on his part. If nothing else, it seemed highly unlikely that she would stick to her word. It would be a blind bargain on his part, and he could hardly file suit against her in a court of law if, having being properly slept with, she should decide to break her contract and stay in Coldwater. And she didn't seem the type to give up a profitable and, evidently, an enjoyable business just to keep a bargain.

So to hell with it. Something was wrong and he didn't want to think about it. And, because his mind would turn nowhere else, it looked as though there was only one conceivable way to get his mind off the subject at hand.

And, accordingly, he leaned over and stroked the bare back of his wife until she awoke.

They made a warm and delicious sort of love, with her mind still drugged by sleep and her body only partially awakened. He took the softness of her into his arms, and he kissed her closed mouth, and he pulled her tight to him and felt passion blaze through him like a sword through silk.

It was animalism, pure and simple. They made a very direct love, a very sweet-and-simple love, and they made it with no tension and no pretense and no frills. When it was over he rolled free of her embrace and fell back on his pillow, and she lowered her head and drifted back into sleep without saying a word. She had not opened her eyes throughout the whole episode.

He tried to sleep but it took some time. And while he lay awake and tried to sleep he spent his time very carefully analyzing the lovemaking he and Lily Sue had just been through. His analysis was as cold and precise as a geologist's analysis of a sample of dirt, and he cursed himself for the fact but couldn't help himself. He thought about what they had done, and he placed each little moan and groan in its proper lot, and the wheels of his mind turned like wheels in a clock, or on a train.

Maybe there's a lot of NYU in me, he thought. Maybe the hill stuff isn't all of it. Maybe I absorbed all the baloney about scientific method.

To hell with it.

But there was one thing which he couldn't escape. For one reason or another, the incident had been somewhat less than satisfactory. He tried to see if it had been different essentially from previous embraces with Lily Sue and he could detect no relevant differences.

Yet before she had always been all he had wanted.

So what was wrong?

He could guess the answer to that one. It was simple enough once you got the knack of looking at it, like trying to shoot a fish from on top of the water. In school they taught you it was something called refraction, meaning the rays of light bent when they struck the water surface. In Arkansas nobody knew about refraction; they just knew that to hit the damn fish you had to aim a little ways away from him.

Thinking could work the same way. So he thought sort of over to one side, like with a big cat floating near the surface, and he saw something which he did not want to see.

Point one—Lily Sue had been plenty for him, and now something was missing.

Point two—Lily Sue had not changed.

Therefore: what he wanted was no longer the same.

And that meant several things. It meant that his marriage might change if he didn't watch himself. And it meant that some little part of him wanted what Jan Partridge had to offer.

He shuddered violently. Then his mind forced all thoughts away and he went to sleep.

AFTERNOON.

"You just wait an' see," Royal Peters was saying. "You would of spent this money, girl. You would of thrown it away on doodads and geegaws. But this money won't get thrown away. I'm gonna hold it in close for you."

Sure you are, Lizzie thought. You're a real sweet old sweet man, Royal. You'll spend it on a big long car and dollar cigars and hundred-dollar suits and ten-buck shirts. You'll spend it is fast as I make it, and I wouldn't put up with you for a minute if I had a brain in my damn head.

"Just take a little time," Royal said. "Then we get ourselves a little stake put together. A little bread saved up. Then we go into business."

We're already in business, she thought. A real groove of a business. I turn the tricks and you wind up with the bread. A fine business for you and no business at all for me. No business for a lady, by God.

"You know what we going to do?"

We're going to fly, she thought. You tell me how we're going to fly. You make me all the promises in the world. And I'll believe them, Royal. I'll believe every lie you tell me—how we get out of this business and into something respectable, how we made money and raise kids and we're married and everything. You lay it on thick as thick can be, and this girl will believe every last lying word you tell her. Because she wants to believe it so bad she can't help it, even when she knows it's a lie.

"You didn't answer me, girl. Lizzie, girl—you know what we're going to do?"

"What, Royal?"

"First off, you tell that white trash Jan, that madam, you tell her to go to hell. That'll be a kick, won't it now? Just tell her to go to hell."

She nodded to him. Sure, she thought. Tell Jan to go to hell. That would be the day.

"Then the two of us, we go to a courthouse and take ourselves out a license. A marrying license. You think you could stand that, girl? Marrying me?"

She told him how wonderful it would be.

"Then we take that money," he said, warming to the

subject. "We take that money, all that money you would of wasted but I'm saving it up for you, and we go up to Ohio where it's a little more like civilization, and we buy ourselves a little restaurant. Nothing fancy, girl. A little lunch counter and a couple of three tables. I do the cooking and you do the waiting on table and we make out. We make out good."

She looked into her mind and she actually saw that lunch counter. She saw the spanking white Formica top, and she saw the tables with red and white checkered table cloths, and she saw the floor cleanly swept and a huge coffee urn filled with boiling hot coffee. She pictured Royal scrambling a batch of eggs with grits, Royal wearing a chef's hat, and at first the picture was ridiculous. She pictured herself with a pencil behind her ear and a nice clean apron on, and that picture too was ludicrous, comical.

But the more she looked, the more her eyes stared into her brain, the more sensible that picture became.

"Couple of kids. Can't have a family without kids now, can we?"

She added two children to the picture. A boy first, and then a girl. The boy maybe two years older than the girl, so he could watch out for her and take care of her. The brother she herself had never had.

"And we settle down. No more wrong side of the law. We join the AME church and the N-double-A-C-P and vote the Democratic ticket and keep our noses clean. Before you know it the kids'll be married and you'll be a grandma, all fat and cute and white-haired. A whole lifetime together. Think you can stand Royal for a lifetime, girl?"

She nodded again. The whole routine—respectability, love, children. That's what they always promised. With Royal it came in the form of a lunch counter. With Lucian it had been a bar and grill in a good neighborhood. With another sweet man it was a bowling alley.

Always promises. And the promises all followed the same pattern, the pattern of wait and see and as soon as we have enough money will we have fun. The pattern of promises that, unhappily enough, never came true.

She wondered for a moment whether Royal was playing it by ear or if maybe there was a handbook for pimps, a sweet man's bible that told you how to sweet-talk a girl, how to build her up way to the moon and then let her hang there forever.

Or maybe he really meant it, in his own strange way. Maybe he dreamed that no matter how much money he spent they would miraculously come out far ahead of the game, and that at that time he *would* marry her and they *would* move to Ohio and they *would* buy that restaurant and raise those kids and everything else that went with the dream. Maybe he was hanging on a hook much the same as the one she was on, waiting for his ship to come in, for his dream to come true.

And maybe, just maybe, the dream would come true.

Here you go, half her mind said. Here you go, you crazy

black pigeon. Up in the air again. Dreaming again. He feeds you a pack of lies and you swallow them whole, don't even chew them a little. What kind of cigarettes have you been smoking, girl? What kind of cloud are you floating on?

Shut up, the rest of her said. Because it's a good live dream and it's going to come true. It's peace and happiness and goodness and gladness and this time, this time out of all the times, it is going to come true.

Maybe wishing would help it. Maybe if she wished just as hard as she could it would come true.

She wished as hard as she could. And, though the other half of her mind was laughing like hell, she didn't listen to it.

THIS MAN'S NAME WAS Cyril Snope and he was drunk.

Now this may not be an absolutely accurate description. Accurate, perhaps. To say that Cyril Snope was drunk, however, is to lack precision. There are degrees of drunkenness and there are types of drunkenness, and Cyril Snope would not by any means have fit all of these categories.

There is giggling drunk and there is staggering drunk and there is falling-down drunk. There is happy drunk and there is sad drunk. There is drunkenness which means immobility, where the drunk could no more raise his arms over his head than he could fly. There is mental drunk, where the man can walk and talk perfectly well while his mind sails in an orbit all its own.

Cyril Snope was none of these. He was mean drunk.

Which is to say that he was drunk and he was mean, a not uncommon state for Cyril. He was thirty-three years old, a big hunk of Kentucky manhood with pig eyes and a bloated stomach and a peanut brain. He was a relatively rotten louse when cold sober, and when he was drunk he was a total bastard.

Tonight he was a total bastard.

He was also paying a visit to the trailer. It was a Thursday night, a calm and placid Thursday night, a relatively slow Thursday night, and Cyril Snope walked into the trailer at a quarter to ten. He didn't seem to be drunk—if he had, Jan would have ordered him to leave and would have called the police if he refused. But he was completely in control of himself and he fooled Jan into thinking he was cold sober.

He stood in the office and looked first at Jan, then at Lizzie, finally at Marna. Andy was in a room turning a trick and thus was unavailable for inspection. He looked the three girls over very carefully, taking plenty of time to make his choice.

"All right pretty," he said. "Three pretty gals. Tough to choose."

All three smiled.

"This-here Blondie, though," he said, tossing his head to indicate Marna. "This looks extra fine. All nice and soft and warm. You as soft as you look, Blondie?"

Marna giggled.

Cyril Snope made his decision. He took a crumpled

ten-dollar bill from the pocket of his gabardine windbreaker and unfolded it, smoothing out the wrinkles with care. He handed the bill to Jan.

"I'm taking little Blondie," he announced. "On account of she looks so soft and warm."

And he took Marna's arm and led her into her room.

At that point, the heretofore camouflaged mean-drunk part of Cyril Snope took control of the situation. Marna began to go through her paces simply enough. She kicked off her shoes and tugged her dress over her head. This left her naked, and she stood waiting while Snope's eyes took in the full beauty of her body from head to feet.

"Looks warm," he said. "And soft, too. Pillow soft."

She shifted her weight from one foot to the other. He moved closer to her and she waited for him to touch her His hands reached out and she plastered the automatic smile on her face.

He took a breast in each of his big hands.

"Soft," he said. "Real soft. Warm, too. I like it when a woman's soft and warm."

He dropped his hands. The fingers of his right hand curled slowly until they made a fist. She looked at his hand, not understanding at all, and his fist moved back and then forward. He hit her with all his strength in the precise center of her belly.

All the air rushed out of her. There was nothing in the world but a ripping blood-red pain in her stomach and she doubled up in agony, her hands clutching the sore spot and her knees buckled beneath her. She couldn't even scream. The pain squeezed the breath out of her and she couldn't get it back.

"Now you keep real quiet," he said. "You're soft and warm and that's all the way it's supposed to be. Now you keep quiet, because as soon as you make a damn sound I'll kill you. I ain't kidding. I'll kill you deader'n hell."

She looked at his eyes, his filthy little pig eyes, and she knew that he was not kidding.

He would kill her.

He stripped the pillow-case from the pillow, then tore it effortlessly into strips of cloth. He put two of these into her mouth and tied them tight for a gag. She tried to say something and found that no words came out. She tried to breathe through her mouth and couldn't.

"Now we have fun," he said.

His idea of fun and Marna's private and personal idea of fun did not happen to coincide. His idea of fun, as a matter of fact, was her idea of agony.

Three times he hauled her to her feet and hit her with all his strength in the pit of the stomach. Each blow was worse than the one preceding it, and when he hit her the third time she blacked out. The pain was too much—she lost consciousness.

When she came to she was lying on her back on the bed and he was seated next to her, a vacuous grin on his ugly face. He reached for her, and once again he took a breast in each of his big hands.

This time he squeezed.

Hard.

Very hard.

She screamed against the gag but not a sound got through. His hands were making her breasts turn to jelly and she couldn't stand the pain. He released them for a moment, and then he squeezed again, and once more she tried to shriek and failed.

He laughed at her. "Nice," he said. "I'm glad I picked you, Blondie. You're soft as feathers."

He beat her breasts with his fists and she wondered if she was going to live, if there would be anything left when he was through. He beat her black and blue, and when she thought that one more blow would surely kill her he stopped suddenly and tore his own clothes off.

Then he fell on her and made violent and sadistic love to her, his hands flailing at her breasts while he did so.

After it was over, all the while he dressed himself and lit a cigar, she could not move. She lay in one position. She didn't hurt any more. She was too used to pain to feel anything. Instead she was numb all over, and she wondered if the numbness was a permanent thing, if perhaps it would last her for the rest of her life.

And he insisted upon talking to her.

"Best in a long time," he said. "Best and warmest and

softest girl in I don't know how long. Glad I picked you, Blondie. We had a hell of a time."

Nothing but pain and achingness. Nothing but agony, nothing but misery.

Nothing else.

"Have to come back and see you again. Have to try you on for size. Bet you'll be glad to see me, Blondie. Bet you haven't had anything like this in a long time, huh?"

Why didn't somebody help her? Where was Jan? Where was Andy?

Where, for that matter, was Will? Will would help her. Will would get rid of the sadist.

"Only one thing," Cyril Snope said. "You're about as soft as anybody could want, but you might be a little bit warmer. Wouldn't hurt at all. Can't have a girl too warm. The warmer a girl is, the better she is."

She didn't realize what was coming until it came. She saw him take his cigar from his mouth and she saw him move closer to her. Then she saw the cigar move to the peak of one big firm breast, and then she felt the heat as it came closer.

Then he pressed the glowing tip of the cigar down upon her nipple.

The pain was a wholly new experience. It eclipsed everything, and the only merciful part of it was that it didn't last forever. It was too intense to be endured for long. She gave one hideous scream which the gag concealed from the world—and then she passed out.

Chapter 7

CYRIL SNOPE CLOSED THE door behind him and walked back to the office. "Fine little girl you got there," he said. "Blondie, I mean. Soft and warm and all. Man gets his money's worth around a place like this. I'll be back.".

Jan smiled. "Where's Marna?"

"You mean Blondie? She's dressing, I reckon. Be out momentarily. I'd wait, but I've got some hurrying up to do. Give her a kiss for me."

And Cyril Snope went out the door and walked away into the night.

After five minutes Jan got the feeling that something might be wrong. It does not take five minutes to be back in service. Accordingly Jan walked back to Marna's room and opened the door. She saw Marna lying in bed with her eyes closed and laughed, assuming logically enough that the blonde girl was sleeping. She went over to the bed to wake her.

And screamed.

THE DOCTOR WHO TREATED Marna explained that her injuries would not be permanent, with the possible exception of her burned breast. The end of the cigar had done a little damage to her nipple, and the doctor said that she might have some degree of difficulty nursing a child with that particular nipple. Since it was highly unlikely that Marna would ever have a child much less nurse one, this didn't seem to be the most disabling injury possible.

The doctor prescribed two weeks of rest, two weeks without working. This was a superfluous sort of prescription, since Marna would have had a vacation for that length of time in any event. She was in no condition whatsoever to have relations with anybody, for love or money. From a purely physical standpoint, sex would have been torture.

Then there was the psychological end of things. It didn't take Ziggie Freud himself to figure out that the little trip to Krafft-Ebing Land with Cyril Snope had been a traumatic experience for one Marna Leeds. Asking her to go to a man right about then would have been tantamount to asking Ishmael to chase a few more white whales. A man had made a pretty wreck out of Marna and the male sex in general was something rather loathsome to her for the time being. It only stood to reason.

The police investigation was conducted with diligence, dignity, expedience and, perhaps more than anything else, savoir faire. Jan went to Ernie Perkins at once, explaining in detail just what had happened and giving as precise a description of Snope as she could. Perkins told her he would find out what he could. He found out virtually everything within twenty-four hours and reported to her in person.

"Found that guy for you," he said.

"Who is he?"

"Trash," Ernie Perkins said. "Name of Cyril Snope. Good for nothing."

"Is he in jail now?"

Ernie took out a cigar and lit it. "Meant to ask you about that," he said. "Meant to find out what you might want to do. About Cyril, that is."

"He ought to get his head handed to him."

"The thing is," Perkins went on, "we could jail him and have us a trial for him. But that sort of drags things out into the open. Jury'll do whatever we want, but you need a jury first. And then you need to put that blonde girl on the witness stand and let her talk. That sort of thing don't help you any. Lets the whole world know you're running a house and I know about it."

"Doesn't everybody know that already?"

He chuckled. "It's not official. You see what I mean? It gives the women's groups a whole barrel full of ammunition. Two barrels, that is. And they'll fire both of them at once. Might sort of sink the boat, if you follow me."

She followed him perfectly. A trial would be something of a disaster for the business, and wouldn't accomplish a hell of a lot anyway. But she hated to see Snope come out smelling like a rose. It didn't seem fair. Marna had done nothing and had been rewarded with one hell of a beating. The sadist who gave it to her deserved to get his in return.

She told Perkins this.

"Well," he said. He rolled the cigar from one side of his mouth to the other. "That's a way to look at it. Maybe a good way, I guess. But you got to take account of Snope. He was drunk at the time. Mean drunk."

"That's an excuse?"

"Not saying it is. Now, I could get some of the boys together and we could sort of knock Snope around a mite. Bust him up a little. But that wouldn't be too good."

"Why not?"

"He's got kin, for one thing. For another, the men might not take to the idea of beating up somebody from Coldwater because he got rough with a whore. It's different if we toss a soldier boy around a little. They like you better than the soldiers. But they like their own a damn sight better'n they like you, even if their own is one like Cyril. Might start a mess."

"So we leave him alone?"

Chief Perkins turned palms up. "I talked to him," he said. "I have a doubt he'll be back bothering you again. And any time he gets a skinful I'll slap him in the tank and shove him around a mite. But I wouldn't do more than that. Wouldn't make much sense."

"It still doesn't seem fair."

"Fair is fair," Ernie said. "But fair ain't always sensible. Some of the time, but not always."

She thought it over, and it still didn't seem any fairer.

But he was right, all things considered, and it looked as though she had to go along with him. She didn't much like it, but there was no handy alternative.

THE NATURAL WAY TO consider the beating of Marna Leeds by Cyril Snope would involve a careful examination of the effect of this event upon the community at large—MacNamara Army Base, the trailer camp, the town of Coldwater—in essence, all those social groups which came somehow into contact with Marna. This, however, does not work out too well in practice. The beating of Marna had a very simple effect upon the men who lived in barracks at MacNamara Army Base. They went without the blonde for a period of two weeks. Whatever psychological traumas this might have engendered are difficult if not impossible to determine.

It might be reported that Marna's absence from the lists of combat did slightly overload the trailer on several given nights, with more work available than the three girls ready to do business were able to service. Two men fought as a result, each of them desiring to be first with Jan at the time. Since the two had been spoiling for a fight for three weeks anyway, Marna could hardly be called a prime cause of their quarrel, which was easily settled anyway when one knocked the other unconscious with a right cross to the forehead.

The effect upon the town was comparable. For one thing, the town did not get much word on what had transpired, since neither Cyril Snope nor Marna Leeds were particularly disposed to boast over the incident. A good many townspeople found it eminently possible to lead normal and rewarding lives without knowing the slightest damn thing about the affair. Those who did know what had happened—and they formed a decided minority of the population of the town—didn't attach much significance to it. As far as they were concerned, it was sort of a damn shame since the girl hadn't hurt anybody. They dismissed it as another point proving that Cyril Snope was a worthless and ornery bastard, which was something they had known all along.

Some of them also suspected that Marna herself was not entirely without blame. They guessed that she had probably done something to provoke the act, with possibilities advanced ranging from complex sexual acts she had refused to perform to complex acts which she had insisted upon. One man staunchly supported the theory that Marna had laughed at the quality and quantity of Cyril, and this theory was gaining acceptance until one citizen with inside information (he had gone swimming with Cyril once) explained that this could not possibly be the case.

In the trailer camp itself, a little more interest evolved. Men discussed the incident among themselves, with one explaining to another that "some townie bastard beat the hell out of the blonde whore at Jan's trailer." This was occasionally followed up by the explanation that the girl was "you know, the big hunk Will Taylor's been chasing after."

Husbands occasionally relayed the information, or part of it, to their wives, but the women did not discuss the issue among themselves. All in all, the episode did little more than to confirm already existing suspicions that townies were rotten to the core, which was something virtually everyone had taken more or less for granted from the beginning.

The fact that everyone in the camp seemed to act as though Cyril Snope was not a rather specialized form of pervert but just an extreme type of townie did not do anything to improve the disposition of Lily Sue Appleton. She had been born and raised in Coldwater and she was proud of it. When she married Jack Appleton, she became sort of a link between the two opposing forces. Now the link was being tested. It seemed as though every day served only to set the town against the camp and the camp against the town. Lily Sue was caught in the middle—loyal to her husband on one side and her father on the other, to her new friends on the one hand and her old on the other.

The new development didn't help. Since she probably loathed all the girls in the trailer more than any of the other army wives—after all, her own husband's ex-wife was the leader of the damned thing—because of this, she couldn't bring herself to feel an overpowering amount of sympathy for Marna. As far as she was concerned personally, the world would be a lot better off if somebody burned all four of the witches. So when the trailer people talked against the town, Lily Sue felt compelled to take the town's part.

And this, of course, did not help relations between Jack and Lily Sue.

But this type of conjecture beclouds the main issue. In all of the town and the camp and the base, one person more than any other was directly affected by Cyril Snope's brutal treatment of Marna Leeds. This single person had a more direct stake in things than the vagueness of social roles and group conflicts. He was personally involved.

His name, of course, was Will Taylor.

Now to explain what happened with Will is not easy at all. When he heard, of course, the first thing he did was try to see Marna. She loved him, she was mad for him, and he loved her. Something had happened to her and he had to see her.

But she wouldn't see him.

"She's too worn out for visitors," Jan lied. "She'd better stay the way she is now."

"Can't I just look in on her?"

"Better not."

He went away, disappointed. At this point no one knew who the mystery man was, no one but Cyril Snope himself, so all Will could do was wait. He returned the next day, and this time Jan didn't bother lying.

She sent him in.

"Marna," he said, running to her side. "Marna, baby, what happened? What happened to you, honey? Who did it? I'll tear him apart, baby. I'll kill him for you."

She looked at him. Her eyes were very deep, very still. And in a very level tone of voice she told him to get out of the room and never come back.

He couldn't believe it.

"You're a man," she shouted. "And I hate men. You're a goddamn rotten man and I hate you and I don't want to look at you! Get away from me! Get away!"

He couldn't leave the room. Finally Jan sent Lizzie to take him by the hand and lead him out of there. "She's all mixed up now," Lizzie told him confidentially. "Right now she don't want to see you. You ought to stay away from her for awhile, let her come back to herself sort of."

"But she loves me."

"That's right," Lizzie said. "She loves you. But she's been through a lot and she has to have time to straighten out. You just go some place and be cool for awhile, huh?"

He nodded brokenly. He walked slowly to the door, his shoulders stooped.

Then he turned.

"How long?"

Lizzie looked at Jan. "Two weeks," Jan said. "Give her the two weeks to rest up. Then come on back if you want to see her. Come back in two weeks."

He nodded again, slowly. "Two weeks," he repeated. "Two weeks."

IT TOOK TWO WEEKS.

Two weeks. Or fourteen days. Or a fortnight, if you

are either British or affected. At any rate, Will Taylor spent two weeks behaving much like a robot. He dreamed his way through those two weeks. He went to the base every day and soldiered competently but without enthusiasm. He lived with his wife, and he tried his best to keep his concern and confusion from showing to her.

He was not entirely successful in this last aspect. Betty Taylor was a sufficiently perceptive girl to tell that something was radically wrong. But there was of course no way for her to connect Will's moodiness with the beating which had been administered to Marna by Cyril Snope. She figured that something was bothering Will, that something was on his mind, and she guessed that it was something he had to keep to himself. If he wanted her to know about it he would tell her. If not, then it was none of her business and she shouldn't be wondering about it.

So for two weeks Will went about the performance of more or less routine tasks and spent his spare time brooding. For two weeks Lizzie Jackson turned her tricks at night and spent her afternoons with Royal Peters. He was still taking all of her money, and he was still promising her the moon in the form of a southern Ohio small town lunch counter, but now she chose to believe everything he said to her.

For two weeks Marna stayed in her room and recovered, slowly but surely, from the beating she had taken. The pain was the least important part of it. More than that was the fear, the dark and nameless fear that woke her up in the middle of the night and made her cry out in empty terror.

For that, there was always Andy.

Andy was an emotional nurse, if that makes any sense. Andy was always there, always ready to comfort Marna when she needed comforting, to stroke her head and speak softly and gently to her, to calm her when the terror struck home. And this was terribly important.

Before Cyril Snope, before the beating, a change had been taking place within the personality of Marna Leeds. Perhaps Andrea realized this more precisely than Marna herself did. In any event, the fact that she was sleeping with Will Taylor on a non-professional basis, the fact that there was an illusion of love present whether or not this illusion had any actual basis in truth, was enough to shift Marna gradually away from lesbianism and toward normal sexuality.

This shift did not happen overnight. It was a gradual thing. Bit by bit she found herself looking forward more and more to Will's appearance each evening. Bit by bit she found herself gaining enjoyment from making love with him. And, at the same time, her need for Andrea began to diminish.

It was elementary. For once she was sleeping with a man without getting paid for it. The association of heterosexuality with payment was broken, and she was more nearly able to adjust to normality. She did not need Andrea so much, and Andrea's lovemaking seemed almost childish.

Now this was changed.

Cyril Snope had changed it. Cyril Snope, by beating her and violating her, by pressing the tip of his cigar to the tip of her breast, had managed to undo everything that Will Taylor had begun to accomplish.

Cyril Snope was a man.

He had hurt her.

Therefore, obviously, men hurt you. And Will too was a man, and he too was not someone to love but someone to fear, not someone to take pleasure with but someone to exploit. Once again she needed Andrea, needed her deeply and desperately. Once again the mere fact that a man was a man was enough to make her hate the thought of spending more than a few minutes in his company. Once again sex with a man was set up as something to be endured for the remuneration, not something to enjoy.

Once again Marna Leeds was a lesbian.

ANDREA MILHOUS WAS NOT exactly an innocent bystander during those two weeks. The months spent working for Jan had hardened her, and the days when Marna "didn't feel like it" had sharpened her, and Andrea Milhous was no longer the feather-headed New York call girl who had made the trip to Coldwater in the first place. She was shrewder now, and more calculating, and she had developed a way of deciding what she needed and then going after it in the best possible manner.

What she needed now was Marna. She needed Marna

if for no other reason than that Marna was the only other lesbian beside herself in all of Coldwater. That would have been reason enough for Andy, but the added fact that she happened to be in love with the blonde sort of helped things along.

Her love did not negate the fact that she was ready to lure Marna back into lesbianism by any and all means, fair and foul. All was supposed to be fair in love and war, and Andy saw no reason why one's love for another person should prevent one from using sneaky tactics in ensuring the return of that love.

Why not, damn it?

"Marna," she would say, while she massaged the back of the blonde girl's neck, "there's only one way to treat a man. You've got to take him for everything he's got. That's the way it's set up, cookie. The boys want it and the girls sell it to them."

Marna would look doubtful, but just for a moment. Then she would agree.

"Men are bastards," she would go on, setting up the connection, letting it roll onward and upward like an anti-grav snowball. "Look what they did to you."

"They?"

"Sure. The two of them."

"Two of them?"

"That Cyril bastard," Andy said. "The one who beat you. And that other one."

"Who?"

She pretended to think. "I forget his name," she said, careful to let Marna supply the name. "You know which one I mean, don't you?"

"Will?"

"That's the one," Andy said. "The bastard who tried to con you into falling for him."

And, because she had been set up properly, Marna laughed. "Oh, that was just a come-on," she said. "That was Jan's bit. He was the one who got it in the neck on that routine. Jan paid me for every trick I turned for him. We were just setting him up as a patsy to ruin his marriage. It's a thing Jan has."

Andy relaxed. That was fine. It was also true, but it was a fact Marna had managed to forget for awhile. Now she was remembering it, remembering that in truth she was a lesbian and Will was an empty-headed trick she couldn't possibly give a damn about.

"Whatever it is," Andy said, "the dumb hick thinks you love him."

And Marna laughed again. "To hell with him," she said. "To hell with Will Taylor. He'll be coming back pretty soon, coming to see me. Then I can tell him just how crazy I am about him. I'll tell him to go screw the moon!"

Andy smiled. "You tell him," she said. "You fix him good, sweetheart. You teach him."

And she stretched out on the bed and took Marna.

WILL TAYLOR TOSSED IN his bed.

Another night, he thought. Another night and he would be able to see her. Another night and he could find out what was the matter, and do something about it, and then everything would be all right again. No more standing and sitting and staring like a wooden Indian in front of a cigar store. No more bland nothingness, eating food without tasting it, smoking cigarette after cigarette until his mouth was stale and his lungs were soot-coated from the smoke. No more of that.

Because his mind was made up now. Maybe this was what it took, this nothingness. Maybe when a man was forced to sit down with himself and think things out he could make up his mind the way it had to be made up. Whatever it was, he had made his decision. And he was sure it was the right one.

He was going to divorce his wife and marry Marna.

Well, he wouldn't exactly divorce his wife, of course. He'd get her to divorce him, because that would be the nicer way of doing things. And then he'd have Marna, and it wouldn't be a one-way relationship but something that could blossom into something beautiful. He wouldn't have to share her with other men, to toss in his sleep with the picture of other men's hands on her body.

It was strange that this had never bothered him much before. In some fashion his mind had been able to accept all this, to take Marna on her own terms and accept her prostitution as nothing more than a job. The beating had changed all that, just as it had magnified his love for her to the point where he wanted her all to himself forever.

Now he couldn't picture Marna with another man—any man—without feeling fury's iron grip around his belly and hate surging within his bloodstream, a blind and nameless hatred for the faceless nameless man with her. At least she wasn't working during those two weeks, he thought. That was some consolation. He couldn't see her, but neither could anybody else. And tomorrow he would see her and after that she would be his.

His. All his. Permanently.

He tried to imagine what it would be like to be married to a girl like Marna. It would be different, he told himself. All the pleasures of companionship that he got with Betty, plus all of Marna's magnificent ability in bed. It would be something everybody dreamed about and nobody got.

It would be perfection.

It would be his.

All his.

And he only had to wait one more day, one tiny day that would be over almost before he knew it. Then it would be time. Time to see her, time to talk to her, time to tell her. Time to break the news as gently as possible to Betty, and time to break it as jubilantly as possible to Marna, and time to take her warmth into his arms and hold the sweetness of her close to him.

Time.

Plenty of time.

He closed his eyes for perhaps the three thousandth time that night. Closed them in the darkness and willed his mind to relax. It didn't help, particularly. No will power he thought stupidly. Will has no will power.

Tomorrow, he thought.

Tomorrow.

Chapter 8

JAN SAW HIM FROM a long way off. She saw him walk with a lazy but purposeful stride, a way of walking that seemed slow and easy but one that covered a great deal of ground. His head was tossed back a slight degree and his arms moved at his sides. It was a lean and lanky way of walking, a shucks, ma'am, I'm just a country boy way of walking, and as she watched him approach she realized very suddenly just why she wanted to destroy him.

He walked like Jack.

That, in the shell of a nut, was it. He walked precisely like Jack, and although he didn't look like Jack very much, he all at once seemed similar in a huge number of ways. He was a small-town boy too, and he had a wife, and he was ditching the wife because he was in love with a tramp.

That, of course, was why she had wanted to destroy him all along. He was Jack, and his wife was Jan, and Marna was Lily Sue Finch. That was the psychological symbolism, if you wanted to get all symbolic and cute about it.

Only this time the outcome was going to be different. This time, instead of the man getting all the cream, the man was going to get his face rubbed in it. This time, instead of

Will winding up with Marna as Jack had wound up with Lily Sue, Will was going to get his head kicked in by Marna. Then he could go skulking home with his tail tucked securely between his legs—and she meant that quite literally—and then his wife could toss him out too, and then he could go to hell for himself.

Good.

Very good.

Excellent, in fact. He was going to get his, and this was one little production that had been stage-managed and directed by one Jan Partridge, madam extraordinary, from beginning to end. Well, not quite from beginning to end, she amended. The Cyril Snope bit part had not been in the script. But it had come in handy, and had only served to crystallize what she herself had arranged.

She walked to the front of the trailer and opened the door for him. She gave him a big smile and laughed to herself behind it.

"Bet you're here to see Marna," she said.

He nodded jerkily.

"You go right on in," she told him. "She's all alone. I guess you might say she's waiting for you."

"Is she feeling better?"

"Oh, she feels fine," Jan said. "Better than ever. The rest was good for her."

"She's perfectly all right?"

Jan nodded, grinning. "There's only one thing she's

missing," she told him. "And I think it's something you can supply, so go right on in."

That was all he needed. He hurried past the office, heading for Marna's room, and Jan also left the office and went to her own room. She did this for two reasons. For one, her room shared a wall with Marna's, a thin wall, and she wanted to be able to hear everything that went on in there.

For another, she had the feeling that it wouldn't be a bad idea to keep out of Will Taylor's way when Marna brought his world down around his ears.

HE WALKED INTO THE room after she had answered his knock. She was just as he had pictured her. She lay on her bed, stretched out on her back, stark naked. She was the goddess of sexual love, the symbol of everything a man and a woman could be to one another. She was magnificent.

"Marna," he said.

She spoke. But her voice was different than he had remembered it, different than it had ever been before. There was an ugliness to it, a rasp, that had not been there previously.

"Get the hell out, Will. No more free rides, honey boy. No more free trips."

He backed away, suddenly unsure of himself. He didn't understand it, couldn't understand it. He understood only that something was radically wrong.

She sat up, legs parted over the edge of the bed, breasts

standing out true and proud from her chest. Her skin was milky white.

"What did you come for, Will?"

"To see you."

She laughed harshly. "That a new word for it. You came to get into me, didn't you?"

His mind was spinning in circles. "I love you," he said. "That's what I came to tell you. I'm going to get Betty to give me a divorce and then we can be married."

Her laughter split the room into schizoid fragments. He backed away again and his hands shook at his sides.

"I don't understand," he said.

"Love," she said.

"Marna—"

"That's another new word for it," she said. "You love me. That means you like the way I play in bed, doesn't it?"

He stared.

"You want to try me on for size, you can damn well pay for it. Ten dollars will do it for you just like anybody else. And you don't even have to divorce your goddamned wife. Just pay your ten dollars. Or twenty dollars, if you want special service. Want something special, honey?"

She did a burlesque dancer's bump and grind and he winced at it. This wasn't Marna. This wasn't the girl he was in love with, the girl who was his whole world. There was a mistake somewhere.

There had to be.

Now Marna was pouting. "What's the matter, honey? You've been to bed before. What's wrong? Wasn't it any fun for you? Didn't you have a good time with me?"

"You know I did."

"So what's the trouble? Aren't I worth ten dollars?"

He couldn't answer. He had so many things to tell her, so many words and phrases he'd gone over time and time again. But now all the words stuck to the roof of his mouth and none of them were worth saying.

He wasn't sure what the trouble was. He didn't know what was happening and his mind was so thoroughly tied up in knots that he couldn't so much as attempt to think straight. He stood there, awkward and gawky, shifting his weight from one foot to another and waiting for the clouds to lift, waiting for the sun to shine, waiting for everything to be all right again.

"You men," she said. "When it's free it's fine and dandy, but as soon as you have to pay for it you freeze tighter than an old maid schoolteacher. Unbutton the wallet, buster. Shell out with the sawbuck."

"Marna—"

"You got something to say to me? Make it fast, sugar. Time is money in this business. While you're wasting my time I could be putting out for somebody else."

"Marna, you love me."

Laughter.

"Marna, you're in love with me. You love to . . . to sleep with me. Remember who I am?"

"Will somebody-or-other. Who cares?"

"Marna—"

"You really think I love you, don't you? You really think I give a damn if you live or die?"

He stared at her and his eyes went out of focus. Everything was wrong, everything was out of focus, and he couldn't tell what to do next, what to say, how to feel, how to react to anything. He was in a dream, an actor in a dream, and any minute he would wake up and everything would be all right again.

It had to be.

"You love me," he said brokenly.

"Are you kidding?"

"When we . . . made love," he began.

"Love? We didn't make love. We rolled around on a bed. It had nothing to do with love."

"Love," he repeated. "It wasn't just . . . business."

"The hell it wasn't. That was all it was."

"But it didn't . . . didn't cost me anything!"

She shrugged. "I thought it would be good advertising."

"You're crazy, Marna." He drew a deep breath and let it out slowly. "You enjoyed it, Marna. You enjoyed it because you were in love with me. I don't know what's the matter with you now. It must be because of the beating that bastard gave you. But you're not talking any sense at all."

"You think I enjoyed it with you?"

"I know damn well you did."

Her laughter was loud and discordant. "Then hang onto your hat," she told him. "Because I got news for you."

"What kind of news?"

"You never showed me a thing, Willie boy."

"But—"

"Shut up and let me finish." She stood up and held her breasts in her hands. But somehow the action did not make her look enticing at all, he thought. There was something profoundly sexless in her approach now.

"You never showed me a thing," she repeated. "No man ever did. You know why?"

He waited.

"Because you're a man," she said, spitting the words at him. "Because you're a goddamned useless man and men just aren't my kick. I don't like men, Willie. A man is something to make money with and that's all."

He didn't understand. He stood there feeling foolish and he waited for her to explain.

She explained.

"You know what I am, Will? Take a good look. Like what you see? Like these boobs? Like this?"

He didn't say anything.

"You're looking at a lesbian, Will." She smiled, letting the words sink in. He stared hard at her and her smile grew.

"A lesbian," she repeated. "A dyke. A gay girl. A lady lover. You know how I get my kicks, Will? I sleep with another girl. We make love together. That's what lovemaking is—not sweating and heaving with a filthy man on you."

"No," he said dully.

"You don't believe it? It's the truth, sugar. This girl and I get in bed, see, and we kiss each other. And it's fun. I kiss her on the mouth and I kiss her breasts and I kiss her legs and she does the same to me. We have a lot of fun, Will. So now you know what I am. I'm a whore and I'm a lesbian, and what in hell have you got to say to that?"

He had nothing to say. Nothing at all. He backed away from her, his brain whirling like a centrifuge, and he tried to take everything that he knew and arrange it in something resembling order. He couldn't. Everything was wrong, everything was out of focus, everything was going haywire. He tried to add it up and he couldn't manage to do so.

Everything was wrong.

"A lesbian," she said. "And you thought I was in love with you. I must have given a damn good performance. I must be one hell of a whore, to make you think that. I guess I'm a pretty good whore, wouldn't you say?"

His hands turned to fists. He took a step toward her and she burst into her strident laughter again.

"That's right," she said. "Hit me. That's what men do. Men hit you. Men beat a girl up because it makes them feel all strong and masculine. Beat me up, Will. It'll make you feel like a million dollars. Give me a real beating. Take a cigar and burn my breasts with it. Then you can tell all your friends what a big he-man you are. You can be proud of yourself."

And she laughed again.

His arms dropped. His hands relaxed. He lowered his head, then turned slowly away from her.

He walked to the door.

"Aren't you going to stick around, Will? What's the matter? You can afford the ten dollars, Willie boy. And you've had me, so you know I'm worth the money. Don't be cheap, Will. Stay around. I'll give you a real good time."

He opened the door and walked out. He closed the door behind him, but even with the door closed he could hear the jangle of her laughter.

It followed him out of the trailer and buzzed in his brain while he walked back to the trailer camp.

SHE WASN'T THE SAME girl.

That was it, he thought. She had been his—sweet, warm and wonderful. And, no matter what she said, she had been in love with him. The lesbian routine was nonsense, sheer nonsense. She had been Marna, his own Marna, his wonderful Marna, and she had loved him just as he had loved her. It was that way no longer.

That was the way it had been.

All because of one man, he thought. All because of a rotten pervert who had turned her from his Marna, his woman, his love, into something else entirely. Before she had been a goddess in human form. Now she was more of a reincarnation of the devil with breasts instead of horns, a female Satan.

Different.

Not his Marna. Not the girl he had loved, not the woman he was planning on making his wife.

This was a different woman entirely.

And one man was responsible for the transformation. One man had very literally ruined her, and unleashed his perversion upon her and had managed to change her from something divine to something satanic. One man had beaten her and tortured her, and her hatred for this man had been multiplied and augmented until it had turned into a hatred for all men.

Including Will Taylor.

He walked back to the camp. His mind seemed to him to be functioning very clearly now, with the mental wheels revolving cleanly and efficiently, with the right connections being made with no effort whatsoever on his part. He saw quite logically what he had to do, what had to be done. All at once it was very simple. It was just a matter of following things through. That, obviously, was all there was to it.

His trailer was empty when he got to it. Betty had gone somewhere that night—he couldn't remember just where, but he supposed it was over to some other trailer for a game of cards or something comparably trivial—and he was glad that she wasn't around. He did not want company.

He walked into the bedroom, went to the dresser and opened the bottom drawer. The .45 automatic was in the back of the drawer beneath several shirts. He loaded it with a fresh clip of six bullets and slipped it under the waistband of his trousers.

One man.

One perverted man, one rotten man, one wretched and devilish and horrible man.

One man.

Named Cyril Snope.

He took out the gun, looked at it, took a deep breath and let it out slowly. Just a gun, he thought. Just a little old gun with six little old bullets in it.

Six presents.

Gifts.

Gifts for Cyril Snope.

He tucked the gun in place again, and pulled his wind-breaker around to cover it, then zipped the jacket shut. He walked out of the bedroom, out of the trailer, and shut the trailer door with something akin to finality.

Then he began walking toward town.

He had never met Cyril Snope. He did not know who the man was, what he looked like, anything about him. He only knew that this man was responsible for everything that had happened to Marna, and that was enough.

He was going to kill him.

He walked to town with a firm, steady stride. His arms did not swing at his sides but simply hung there, studies in grim determination. His woman had been ruined and he was going to avenge her. A man had assaulted his beloved, had wrecked her mind and her body, and he was going to even the score.

Hate.

Blind hate.

It was around eleven at night when he hit town and began walking quickly and steadily down Water Street. Most of the citizens of Coldwater were at home, either watching television or making love to their spouses, or sleeping soundly. Will Taylor walked along, not sure just what he was looking for, sure only that he was going to find Cyril Snope and that, when he did, he was going to kill him deader than hell.

A man was standing under a streetlamp. A short, squat man with dark hair.

Cyril Snope?

Will unzipped his jacket, got his hand around the .45. He walked up to the man.

"Hey," he said.

The man looked up.

"You Cyril Snope?"

The man shook his head. "Nope," he said. "That I ain't."

"You're lying," Will said.

"No cause to lie," the man said. "No cause to lie at all. If I was Cyril Snope I'd own up to it, like as not. But I ain't, so I guess I have to say that I ain't. Since you asked me and all. If you hadn't of asked I wouldn't have said a damn thing one way or the other."

"You're lying," Will repeated, sure of himself now. This man was Snope, no question about it.

He took out the gun and let the man have a look at it.

"Say now," the man said.

Will shot him.

The bullet struck the man in the throat. Whatever he had been about to say was thus lost forever, because the man was dead at once. The bullet entered in more or less the precise center of his throat, and it made a big hole on the way in, and it made an even bigger hole on the way out.

And the man was dead.

Very dead. In almost no time at all the short squat man was lying on the pavement with an inordinate amount of blood around him. Windows went up and doors opened.

"Hey, you!"

Will turned around. A lanky man in uniform was walking toward him, a policeman, one of Coldwater's finest. The man was under the command of Ernie Perkins.

Of course, Will thought. He had made a terrible mistake. The man he shot was not Cyril Snope at all. Cyril Snope was a policeman.

This man coming toward him, *this* was Cyril Snope.

"Hey," the man said.

Will raised the gun.

"Hey!"

The man went for his gun. He moved in slow motion, and his actions were a burlesque of the Hollywood fast draw.

His hand went to his holster, which was buttoned shut. He unbuttoned the holster, took hold of the gun, and had trouble getting it free. It was stuck in the holster.

It was still in the holster when Will shot him.

Will's bullet hit him in the chest, just over the heart, which was plenty. The bullet pierced the artery which led to the head. The man stopped in his tracks and started to put his hand to his chest.

He never made it.

When the hand was almost there the man fell backward, still in slow motion, and crumpled to the pavement. He fell in such a way that his skull cracked open when he hit the ground, and that alone would have been enough to kill him. But he was already dead when that happened, so it actually made no difference at all.

Dead.

Will was pleased now. It had been a shame, shooting the wrong man, but it was all better now. Cyril Snope was dead and he could rest easy. It was unfortunate that it had been necessary to shoot the other man as well, but this was not something that could have been helped. It was all part of the plan. By shooting the other man he had flushed Snope out of hiding, and that was the way it had to be.

You couldn't have everything. You had to take the bad with the good. If you had to kill an innocent man in order to even the score with Cyril Snope, well, that was the way it went.

Anything for Marna. Anything for the girl of his dreams, the girl of his heart, the girl he needed so completely.

Anything.

Then he saw the kid.

The kid was riding a bicycle. The kid was a Negro boy about thirteen years old, a young fellow. The kid was on his way home. He was going to go to bed.

Of course, Will thought. He had made another mistake, a horrible mistake, and it had already cost two lives. He had killed the short squat man, and he had killed the police officer, and in both cases he had made a terrible mistake.

They were not Cyril Snope.

This was Cyril Snope.

This colored kid was the one, the bastard, the pervert, the man who had ruined Marna. He couldn't understand how he made those two mistakes in the first place. Hadn't he known all along that Cyril Snope was colored?

Of course he had.

Of course.

So how had he made the mistakes? One mistake was bad enough. Two mistakes could only be worse. But there would have to be something done about all this. You couldn't go and kill two men for nothing at all.

There had to be a reason. A purpose, a justification, a moral reason for it all.

Cyril Snope had to die.

"Hey," he called. "Hey, Snope!"

The boy turned to look at him. His eyes went wide with terror and he pedaled as fast as he could.

That proved it. If he weren't Snope he wouldn't be trying to get away. The little bastard was Snope and he had done horrible things to Marna, and now he was going to pay for it. Now he was going to get what he deserved, what he had coming to him.

Will took aim. He squeezed the trigger.

The bullet was low. It missed the kid but hit his bike. The bicycle spun out of control and fell in the middle of the street. The kid lay for a moment on the sidewalk, dizzy.

Then he stood up and started to run.

"Snope!"

The kid ran. Again Will Taylor took aim, and again he squeezed the trigger.

This time his aim was a little better. This time the bullet hit the boy in the right leg. The kid—Cyril Snope—let out a horrible shriek and fell to the ground. He was holding onto his splintered leg and trying to run at the same time, and the result was that he stayed where he was, moaning like a stuck pig and squirming around crazily.

That hit him.

Now to finish him off.

There were shouts all around, but to Will Taylor they were just background music. He hurried to the side of the Negro boy and pointed his pistol at him.

Somebody fired a rifle. The bullet whined overhead and

smashed somebody's plate glass window. Broken glass tingled like a million bells.

The kid looked up at the muzzle of the gun. He whimpered terribly and his eyes were saucers in his face.

Will steadied the gun. His hand was shaking now and it was going to be tough to do what he had to do. But he had no choice. This bastard was Snope, the rotten son of a bitch who had ruined his woman. He had to take care of him.

He fired.

The bullet blew up in the kid's face. One moment there was a face and the next moment there was a huge bloody hole where the nose and mouth had been. One moment there had been life and the next moment there was death.

Death.

More bullets, none of which hit Will Taylor. And then, looking at the dead body of the kid he had just shot, *he saw.*

That's the only word for it. For one brief second the veil of insanity was raised up, and he saw. He saw everything sanely and realistically, and no words could describe what he felt.

Five bullets were gone. One for the short, squat man, one for the cop, three more for the Negro boy. There was just one left in the gun.

He put the muzzle of the gun in his mouth. Then he used the one remaining bullet to splatter his tired brains all over the streets of Coldwater.

Chapter 9

THEY BURIED POLICE OFFICER Dick Burton and druggist Edward Niles in Coldwater Cemetery. They buried thirteen-year-old Hollis Rayburn in the colored cemetery, since the good citizens of Coldwater were unshaking in their belief that the races should remain separate in death as in life.

(As a matter of fact, the minister of the Coldwater Baptist Church, Rev. Samuel Taylor Bean, had once preached an elaborate sermon on the theory of two heavens, one white and one black. The twin paradises were, in his view, altogether separate but altogether equal, like schools. He had explained to his audience that their colored brethren were every bit as deserving of their eternal reward, but that they certainly couldn't exist in the same heaven on an equal footing with white folk, and that it would be unfair to make them subservient to the whites. Therefore it followed that two heavens must exist, and it only stood to reason that the good Lord had reasoned along similar lines. The sermon was very well received and had been submitted to a national magazine for publication. The magazine returned it, with a form rejection slip, and Rev. Bean explained that this was the work of the "nigger lovers who run them magazines." But that's by the way.)

At any rate, they buried the three corpses in Coldwater, and they buried Will Taylor back in his own home town. Betty Taylor went into a state of traumatic shock when informed of what had happened. Then one day she packed a suitcase and disappeared. She was never heard from again. The contents of her trailer and the trailer itself were finally sold at auction by the mayor of Coldwater, who divided the proceeds between the survivors of Will Taylor's three victims.

And that was that.

More or less.

"YOU GOT TO GET out of town," Clay Duncan said.

Jan looked at him. She took a long, patient look at the man and tried to decide whether or not to take him seriously. There seemed to be little reason to do so. Clay hardly exerted much influence upon her. Outside of his one outburst of love, he had been quiet and docile enough.

"Why?"

"Because they'll kill you."

"Who will?"

"That's a good question," Clay said. "Everybody wants to. The town and the wives and the married men. They'll stand in line to kill you."

She laughed. "They may stand in line to get a crack at the girls," she said. "They been doing that long enough. But not to kill me. They're more interested in getting what they want in bed than in justice."

"Things can change."

"But they won't."

Clay gave her a cigarette, then lit one for himself. "There's a committee formed," he said.

"They're always forming committees."

"This one might turn out to be different."

"How?"

He shrugged. "Hard to say," he said. "This isn't a regular committee. No chairman, no president, no parliamentary procedure. This is just a group of people who only got one thing in common."

"What's that?"

"They hate you."

"That doesn't bother me a hell of a lot," she said. "I've been hated before. And you know what happens when I get hated? I just get richer and happier and I watch the ones who hate me fall flat on their faces."

"You may not stay lucky forever." He dragged hard on his cigarette, inhaled, blew smoke out. "They don't organize things, this committee. They don't go have a talk with Ernie Perkins. They don't write letters or sign petitions."

"What the hell do they do?"

"Nothing, so far. But something's brewing. Nobody talks about it but you can feel it in the air. It's a bad feeling, Jan. An ugly feeling. A special kind of feeling. Sort of a hunger, really. You know what they're hungry for?"

"What?"

"Violence."

She studied the end of her cigarette. "You would think they've had enough violence," she said. "Will Taylor gave them plenty of violence. Three men and a boy dead as doornails. Isn't that enough for them?"

"They blame that on you."

"Will Taylor was nuts."

"They say you drove him nuts."

"I hardly even talked to him."

Clay shrugged. "I'm just trying to tell you what I think," he said. "I'm just trying to tell you what's in the air. And it's violence or I'm nuts myself. Something's going to happen and you're not going to like it."

"Like what?"

"Hard to say. It might be a lynching. They might burn your trailer. Might run you out on a rail all tarred and feathered and screaming your head off."

She stared at him. "Wake up, for the love of God. This is the twentieth century, isn't it?"

"This is a small town in Kentucky. It's not New York. People here can be pretty damn direct when they got a reason to. And they think they've got a reason."

He lowered his eyes. He picked up his coffee cup and took a sip. "I talked to you about getting out of here together, remember? You and me?"

"I remember."

"Are you any more interested now then you were then?"

She shook her head.

"Well, that's up to you, Jan. I don't want to pressure you into doing anything you don't want to do. If you're not interested in me that's your own business. But if you're not going to leave with me then leave without me. Don't stay here."

"It's that bad?"

"Worse. They'll kill you, Jan. They'll do something bad to you. Whatever you do, you're going to wind up in a mess of trouble. I don't want to see that."

She put out her cigarette and stared at him. "You're full of advice," she said. "But why should you care what happens to me?"

"I don't know," he said.

"You don't know?"

"I guess not." He lowered his voice and looked away. "You're rotten and mean and sneaky, Jan. It's the truth. You're not the nicest person in the world, not by a long shot. Maybe you can't help the way you are. I don't know about things like that."

He caught his breath. "But I know how I feel about you, even if I don't know why. I like you, Jan. I even love you. It doesn't make much sense but I suppose love isn't something that makes sense most of the time anyway. I don't want anything bad to happen to you. I'm afraid it will if you stay here long enough."

AFTERNOON.

The sun was high in the skies, all yellow and hot. The

grass was a sort of green-brown, not like a picture postcard but quite pretty nevertheless and a great deal more natural. They sat on the blanket and smoked, silent cigarettes. They had just finished a picnic lunch—sandwiches and beer—and now they were relaxing, taking life easy.

"I think we should get out of here," Marna said.

"It's early," Andrea said. "Not even two yet. Let's stay for a few more minutes anyway."

"That's not what I meant. I think we should go back to New York. Soon."

"Oh," Andy said.

"I think we should go in a hurry. I don't like it here so much any more."

"You mean after what happened?"

Marna thought it over. "Not just that. Not just about Will and all. That was bad enough, but that's not all."

"Don't blame yourself. He had it coming."

"Maybe he did," Marna said. "But how about the men he killed? And that poor kid?"

"It wasn't your fault, honey?"

"I know. But I want to go home. Back to New York, I mean. That's not the only reason."

"What else?"

"Everything," Marna said.

"Huh?"

"I don't know. It just isn't any . . . any fun here lately. It's a real big drag. The work is a drag and the rest of the time is a drag too. Except when you and I . . . when we made love. That isn't a drag. It couldn't possibly be a drag."

"It's wonderful with us," Andrea said. "And it gets better all the time for us. Better and more beautiful. Have you noticed that?"

"Of course I have."

"I love you, Marna. I love you very much."

Marna leaned toward the brunette. Andy's arms took her, held her, and Andy's mouth came down upon hers. Marna closed her eyes against the glare of the sun and let herself surrender to the kiss. Andy's tongue slipped between her lips and she put her arms around Andy, hugging her close, pressing her own breasts against Andy's.

The kiss lasted a long time.

Then they separated, slowly, and they looked into each other's eyes. "I love you," Marna said. "But there's something wrong even there."

"What do you mean?"

"Oh, I don't know. I suppose nothing, really. Nothing important."

"Tell me."

"I don't know exactly. It's just that making love to you in that dirty room in the trailer, that filthy trailer—"

"I know what you mean."

"It's . . . ugly, Andy. We do it with all those dirty men on the bed and the bed is stained and it's filthy, and then you and I have to make love on it. It wasn't like that in New York. Everything was cleaner."

"I know."

"And people in all the other rooms. Lizzie in her room and Jan in her room. There's no privacy in that trailer, Andy. We don't have any chance to be alone. It's not fair."

"Sometimes I have the feeling that they're listening to us. While we make love."

"Me too. Jan in particular. Sometimes I'll catch her looking at me with this smirk on her face and I can't help guessing what's going through her mind. She's got a pretty dirty mind, the way I see it."

Andy whistled. "The dirtiest."

"And it's not just that she knows we're gay. She knew that all along. The look on her face says more than that. Like she's been listening to us, like she knows what we do, everything. It's kind of filthy."

"I get the same feeling. I don't like her, Marnie."

"I don't like her at all. You know why she's doing this? Why she's running this . . . this cathouse?"

"To make money, I guess. She's making a barrelful. So are we, but she's making twice as much as any of us. Every time we get ten, it's eight for us and two for her. That's in addition to what she gets hustling on her own."

"That's not why she's doing it. It's because she hates the people in the army camp. She wants to ruin their marriages."

"Because of her husband?"

Marna nodded. "It's rotten to work for her," she said. "She does things for the wrong reasons. And I don't like the way things have been going lately. I don't know if you noticed it, but business has been falling off."

"We still get a lot of customers."

"But nobody from the town. And none of the married guys from the trailers. Hardly any, anyhow. Just the single fellows from the base. I got a feeling something bad's going to happen, Andy. Something real bad."

"Maybe."

"And I think we ought to get out. We've got a lot of money saved up. We could afford to go down to Florida for a vacation. Two weeks, say. Two weeks in the sun and swimming on the beaches and just taking it easy. A nice air-conditioned room and good food instead of the slop they have in this jerkwater town."

"And we could dress up a little," Andy added. "And go out at night. And not have any men sweating and panting on top of us at ten bucks a throw."

"And then we'd go back to New York. And we wouldn't have any of this ten buck stuff either. If a guy wants to sleep with us he can pay fifty or a hundred instead of wasting our time for peanuts. That way you get a better class of guy."

"Instead of these slobs."

"You said it. They're slobs here. All of them."

"Let's go."

"When?"

"What's wrong with tonight?" Andy said. "No time like the present. Let's get out of here right away."

"We don't get paid until the end of the week. We'll be losing out on some money."

"So what? To hell with the money. I'd rather be happy than earn an extra fifty or a hundred bucks. Let her keep the money, if it matters to her."

"I guess so," Marna said. "Maybe she'd pay us what we earned so far this week if we told her."

"You kidding?"

Marna shook her head. "You're right," she said. "She wouldn't give us a nickel."

"She'd try to make us stick around," Andy said. "And you know what she's like once she gets talking. She can sell you the Brooklyn Bridge if she puts her mind to it. There's nobody like that girl."

"I know."

"So we better not tell her," Andy said. "It wouldn't do us any good and she'd wind up selling us on the idea of staying for awhile. The best thing we can do is just go without saying a word to her. Just up and leave. Go to Louisville tonight and leave without saying anything and the next thing you know we're under the sun in Florida living the life of Riley."

Marna grinned. Then her face changed. "How'll we get to Louisville?"

"We take a bus. Simple. Then a plane from Louisville. They must have planes there, don't you think?"

"I guess so."

"So that's what we'll do. Don't even bother with a suitcase. The clothes we've got here I wouldn't wear to a dog show anyhow. We'll buy new clothes in Miami. We can afford it."

"We'll just take the money."

"You said it."

"We'll leave at dinner time," Marna said. "Just cut and run and she won't know what happened to us. She won't even realize we're gone until eight o'clock. Can't you just picture her face when we don't turn up? She'll have that silly police chief looking all over town for us, and we'll be living it up in Miami."

They giggled.

"Just one thing," Andy said. "Just one thing before we go. One thing we ought to do."

"What?"

"Make love."

"Where?"

"What's wrong with right here?"

"Here? Out in the open like this?"

"Sure."

"Somebody'll see us, Andy."

"The hell they will. Who's going to be around here now? Besides, it'll be a switch making love in a clean place. It'll be a big change from that filthy little room. And we'll get a nice suntan while we do it."

Marna giggled.

"Don't you want to, baby?"

"Sure I do."

"Then," said Andy, "let's."

"Won't somebody see us?"

"Nobody'll see us."

Nobody saw them.

SOMETHING BAD WAS COMING.

Jack Appleton sat around feeling sick to his stomach. The poker game was something he usually enjoyed, but tonight he couldn't seem to get with it. He was folding winners because he just couldn't take the trouble to concentrate on the game. Normally he was a good card player, but this particular evening he was playing like a low-grade moron.

Because something bad was coming.

That much, he thought, was obvious. All you had to do was sniff the damn air and you wound up smelling trouble. All you had to do was think a little bit and you realized that all hell was going to break loose one of these goddam days. All you had to do was use your head for more than a hatrack and you saw that the whole mess was a keg of powder waiting for one little spark to send it flying to hell.

He picked up his cards. The game was draw poker and he had two pairs, eights over fives. The player to his right opened for a dime. He rode with the bet, met the raise when the dealer bumped a quarter. He and the dealer and the opener were the only players to stay for the draw.

It was getting bad, he thought. Real bad. And the funny

part of it was that he was the only man around who could straighten the whole mess out. He had the keys to it in his hand, and he was sitting around waiting for it to take care of itself.

The opener drew cards. He hesitated for a moment, then decided that two tiny little pairs weren't going to win a damn thing. He discarded the fives along with the odd card and asked for three. The dealer took one.

He put his three cards together with the pair of eights without looking at them. He'd been doing a hell of a lot of thinking lately, even if he hadn't come up with too many answers. There were a couple things he knew damn well, though. One was that Jan had to get out of town or there was going to be trouble, more trouble than the town could stand. Enough trouble to mess up the base, make things rough on the town, and knock hell out of the trailer camp.

Enough trouble to ruin his marriage with Lily Sue.

The opener started the betting with a quarter. Jack spread his cards slowly, looking first at the two eights he had started with, then at a four, then at another eight, finally a second four. He had eights full, a winning hand. He sighed and kicked the bet a quarter.

And he could get Jan out of town. He had thought things over pretty carefully, and he was almost positive that she would be true to her word if nothing else. He had a feeling that she wanted to leave town to begin with but that her pride was stopping her. If he slept with her, the way she wanted, she would have an excuse to leave.

That would do it.

The dealer hesitated, then called the bet. The opener took a long look at his cards, met the raise and kicked a final quarter. Jack decided the man had trips, aces or kings, and was pushing them to the wall. He met the man's raise and raised back, the third and final raise.

He could do it. It was that simple. He could very definitely screw her out of town, because she was dying to get out to begin with.

There was only one trouble.

He was scared.

He was scared stiff, and he was pretty sure he knew what it was that scared him. Simply enough, he was scared he would enjoy it more than he wanted to. He was scared that there was something missing from his relationship with Lily Sue, something that Jan would be able to provide.

This scared him.

The dealer folded his hand. The opener met the raise, calling the bet, and Jack showed his cards. He had a winner. The opener folded his hand without showing it and Jack pulled in the pot. He arranged the chips in stacks.

Afraid he would enjoy it. Afraid that Jan would ruin what he and Lily Sue had and that he would be left with nothing. Well, it was something to be afraid of. It would ruin his life, really. And he didn't want his life ruined.

He thought about Will Taylor. Will's life had been ruined. Ruined, hell—it had been ended. And he could have saved Will's life. If he had gotten rid of Jan when he'd had the chance, Will would never have gone off his nut and killed all those people.

It was his fault.

So what was he supposed to do now? Sleep with Jan and wind up with a busted marriage. Or sit on his behind and wait for the sky to fall in?

He had to do something. He could wait, hoping things would blow over and Jan would leave of her own accord. Or he could get her to leave, hoping at the same time that he would be strong enough to hold his marriage together. He didn't know which choice would prove to be the right one.

But he was fairly sure that whatever he did, it would turn out wrong.

THERE WERE TWO OF them. Two men, one in his early thirties, the other in his late twenties. They were from the town of Coldwater. The older one, Len Assleberg, worked as a janitor at the public school. The younger one, Tom Rainey, clerked in a dry-goods store on Water Street.

They both wanted Lizzie.

"You look here now," Rainey said to Jan. "You charge ten bucks for a go with this-here gal, right?"

"That's right."

"So we'll do better than that," Assleberg said. "We'll give you twenty-five between us. That's twelve and a half apiece. And it won't take no longer either. That's fair, ain't it?"

"Well—"

"I don't want to," Lizzie said.

The three of them looked at her.

"Not natural," she said. "Two men with a girl at the same time."

"So what?"

"I just don't want to."

"Don't know what she's got to be so sniffy about," Tom Rainey said. "She ain't nothing more nor less than a hunk of dark meat anyhow. Ought to be glad of a chance to make twenty-five dollars so easy."

Len agreed.

And so did Lizzie, if against her better judgment. She nodded unhappily and Jan accepted twenty-five dollars in worn five dollar bills from the two men. Then she led them to her own room. Her room now was the room the two girls had shared before they moved out, the two lesbian girls. Since Marna and Andrea had left a few days back, she and Jan both had two rooms apiece, one for work and other for sleeping. It made things a little better, she thought. It was a big drag when you had to sleep where you worked. Harder to fall asleep, if nothing else.

The two men kept up a steady run of chatter which she chose to ignore. She stripped while they studied her, discussing her body aloud as if she was a piece of merchandise on a shelf. Well, what else was she? She was nothing but a piece of cheap goods up for sale and they had bought her. It was their privilege to say any damn thing they pleased about her.

"Now how do you want to do this?" she asked. "One of you watch and then switch?"

"Nope."

"What?"

"Both at once," Rainey said.

"How?"

They told her how. The two separate components were nothing new, of course, but the idea was a fresh notion and one which didn't exactly send her into orbit. But there wasn't a hell of a lot she could do about it. She didn't have any choice in the matter. She was one slave Lincoln hadn't gotten around to freeing, and she was stuck.

They seemed to have their own ideas so she let them work things out pretty much by themselves. The older one came around behind her and put his arms around her, getting his hands on her breasts. She pretended to be excited. She was good at it. She could stand there, cool as ice, not feeling a thing but pretending to, squirming all over the place.

Funny. It was so different when Royal did the same thing to her. These jerks could squeeze her breasts until they melted and it didn't show her a thing. But when Royal ran his hand just ever so lightly over her body she started quivering like an aspen in the breeze.

Funny.

The other one was standing in front of her, and he was running his hands over her, cleverly if ineffectively. She writhed in simulated passion.

"Nothing like dark meat," she heard Rainey say. "Nothing in the world like it."

Sure, she thought. I'm warm as an iceberg, baby. Hot as a turned-off stove. Sure.

But when Royal did the same thing she sailed around the moon on gossamer wings. It wasn't as though Royal's technique was any better. It was pretty much the same, come to think of it. There was no difference between what Royal did to her and what they did to her. There was no difference in the *way* it was done.

The difference was Royal.

And why the hell was that? She couldn't really come up with an answer. When the chips were down, Royal wasn't any better than these two fay bastards. When the chips were down, Royal was a bastard all by himself. The only difference was that he was a spade bastard and they were fay bastards, and that was really no difference at all. By all rules they were as good in and out of bed as he was, maybe better in either or both departments.

Of course there were scenes when she really *believed* that hokey lunch counter bit. And naturally it was a gas then. But how about the rest of the time, when she knew the lunch counter was nothing but a pipe dream, or a stick dream, or maybe a needle dream, but at any rate a dream that was not destined to come true? How about those times?

Something to think about.

Now the two of them wanted to get her to the bed. The older one—Assleberg—led her there while the younger one—Rainey—sort of went along for the ride. She stretched out on the bed and wondered just what they were planning on now. It was going to be difficult to do what they had in mind on a bed. Standing up was more like it.

They showed her.

Assleberg and Rainey both seemed to enjoy it a whole hell of a lot. As for Lizzie, she couldn't have cared less. It was like everything else connected with Coldwater, with the singular exception of Royal Peters.

It was dull.

But she didn't let them go and think it was dull for her. Not by any means. She wriggled like a worm on a hook, and she squealed like a mouse in a trap, and all in all she gave a phenomenal imitation of a woman in the throes of passion.

Her feigned culmination, perfectly timed and perfectly executed would have won her an Academy Award. Her acting was so magnificent that she deserved an Oscar, an Emmy, an Edgar, a Beauregard and a Fag. But, since such awards are not given for the type of performance she gave, she had to be satisfied with twenty-five dollars in its stead.

Eventually it was over. Rainey and Assleberg got up from the bed looking as though they had just finished running the four-minute mile in three minutes. They were obviously exhausted, yet they still managed to strut like bantam roosters. They got dressed, still strutting like bantam roosters, and then they left the room and the trailer.

LATER THAT NIGHT RAINEY and Assleberg sat over beers in a tavern in town. They sat with two other men and they talked about the rolling cathouse that Jan Partridge was running. First they discussed Lizzie Jackson's ability in bed, and they were thoroughly complimentary on that point. There was nothing nicer they could have said for the girl, at least from their point of view.

"Fine little hunk," Len Assleberg said. "I been around some and I don't mind saying it, but I haven't been around so much that I come across something like that every day. And I don't mind saying that neither."

"Hot as a two-dollar pistol," Tom Rainey said. "Nothing hotter, nothing ever. You take a girl like that and you got something with real heat to it, you see."

"It's the type gal she is," Assleberg said. "You get a colored gal, you got something warm and friendly, sort of. One thing, she's so glad to make it with a white man it sends her out of her mind. She knows a white man's something special, you see. It gets to her. It's what they call psycho. All up there in the mind. And it gets down there in something else."

That got a good laugh.

It also called for another round of beer.

"It's a different race," Rainey said. "And don't let anybody tell you that don't make a difference."

Everyone agreed.

"That race," Rainey said, "it's got hotter blood. Fresh from the jungle, sort of."

Everybody agreed.

Eventually the conversation shifted from Lizzie Jackson in particular to the cathouse on wheels in general. And again unanimity of opinion was the rule.

"Bad thing for Coldwater," one of the men said.

"What they call a community eyesore," another man said.

"Ought to shove it off a high cliff," said Len Assleberg.

"Ought to burn it to hell and gone," said Tom Rainey.

Chapter 10

LATE AFTERNOON.

Jan sat in the office with a sheet of paper and a pen on the top of the desk in front of her. She had listed a long column of figures. Originally she had planned on listing expenses and receipts, but in the middle she had grown bored with that and simply listed any number that popped into her head. It was a device to combat boredom at first, then a device to keep her from thinking about topics that disturbed her. On either count it had failed miserably.

It was time.

Time to quit, she thought. Time to throw in the sponge. Time to give it all up. Time to pack up her whorehouse and go home while she was still alive.

She should have listened to Clay, she thought. He had her interests at heart, strangely enough. And she couldn't help believing that, just as he had said, he was in love with her. Admittedly it was a strange love—what other kind of love could a man like him have for a woman like her? But this didn't make his love for her any less real.

Clay didn't come around much any more.

Which only stood to reason. After all, why should he?

She had decided to reject his love, for one reason or another, and through that same love he had developed emotionally to the point where unilateral sex with her was no longer something which he either wanted or needed. So he did not come around much any more, for that she could hardly blame him.

And now it was time to follow his advice. Now it was time to leave Coldwater while she was still alive, while she could still hold her head up. Already two of her girls had left her and the third was so tired of the whole routine that she would be gone any day. It was time to disband the whole operation, to pull up stakes and get the hell out.

She wondered where she was going to go, what she was going to do. She'd wind up in New York probably, she guessed. It was where she belonged. Yet she did not particularly *want* to go to New York, just as she did not especially *want* to go anywhere. She tried to picture herself working at a regular job and the picture refused to make any sense at all.

What would she do?

Vegetate, probably. Get a decent apartment in a decent area and take life easy. Go to plays and nightclubs and spend some of the massive bankroll she had managed to amass. Bide her time, secure in the knowledge that before her money ran out some rich fool of a man would come along to support her as his mistress or, if he was foolish enough, to marry her. She was as attractive as ever, as desirable as ever. And her profession had left no scars on her. Her body was just as it had been and her life of sin did not show in her face. She was attractive to men and she knew how to make them happy. She would never have to worry about money.

She might have to worry about happiness.

She laughed at herself. What was the matter with her? Happiness was a thing called dough, to paraphrase the old song, and she had plenty of it.

Loads of it.

Heaps of it.

Barrels of it.

So why be glum? Why be down in the dumps? All right—in a sense she had failed. She hadn't broken up the marriage of Jack and Lily Sue, which had been one of her main objectives in starting the business in the first place. She hadn't gotten Jack into the same bed with her, either.

But those things didn't seem so damnably important anymore, anyhow.

At any rate, she'd accomplished a few things. She'd helped increase the tension between town and trailer camp. She'd corrupted the police chief a little and she'd made a few wives get along less well with their husbands.

And she'd ruined some lives. She'd sent Will Taylor to an early grave, and he'd taken a few townies along with him. She'd messed up Betty Taylor's life from beginning to end.

That had been an aim of hers. And yet, now that the aim had been achieved, she was altogether highly surprised to discover that she could take no pleasure in the achievement. She had expected an overwhelming sensation of vengeance, had thought it would give her a monumental feeling of accomplishment.

This had not happened.

As a matter of total fact, quite the reverse had taken place. Instead of joy, she had been continually rewarded with sorrow of late. She tried to get happy about what had happened to Will Taylor and she failed. He was a poor little hick from the sticks and she had managed to get him killed. She had also managed to be responsible for the deaths of three persons whom she did not even know, one of them just a kid.

How could you be happy for that?

How could you even want it in the first place?

She took the sheet of paper, the one she had been scrawling a list of numbers upon, and she tore it to paper ribbons. She took her pencil and snapped the point off on the desk, then took the pencil in her two hands and broke it.

It didn't help.

What was wrong with her? What kind of a monster was she, for God's sake? Only a monster could so much as imagine the things she had done. Only a monster could lead the sort of life she had been leading.

A monster.

What had happened to her, really? Her husband had left her for another woman. An all-too-common occurrence, and one that in this instance had to happen. She and

Jack had been hopelessly mismatched from the beginning. It was natural that they should drift apart, natural that he should leave her in time if she did not leave him first.

Her reaction was the only unnatural part of it.

Why had it happened that way? Simple, she thought. Her pride had been hurt. And, because of a simple attack of injured pride, she had struck out in all directions like a cornered rat, hurting everything and everybody within range.

My God, she thought, hit with a strange burst of instant clarity, am I that weak? Am I so unsure of myself?

The answer seemed to be yes.

Well, that settled it. She couldn't get out of the place too soon. It was hard to guess where she would wind up or what she would do, but the sooner she got out of Coldwater, the better it would be for everybody, herself included. The town certainly wasn't the place for her, and it didn't take a genius to figure out that she wasn't doing the town any good. That night, right away, she would pack a suitcase with money and drive her car the hell out of the state of Kentucky.

She took a cigarette from the pack on the desk. She put it between her lips, then scratched a wooden match on the underside of the desk. She let the sulfur part burn, then lit the cigarette and inhaled deeply. She blew the smoke out in a long thin column and tried to collect her thoughts.

Just then she heard a small noise. She turned around and watched the trailer door open. A man came in, a tall thin man with a worried look on his face.

It was Jack Appleton.

"I'm ready," he said.

For a long moment she couldn't understand what in the world he was talking about. He stood there, his face hanging out, and he told her he was ready. Was he nuts? Was the whole world going noisily mad?

"I guess there's no other way," he went on. "And it has to be done. So I'm ready, if the offer still holds."

Light began to dawn.

"If it'll get you out of town, I'll go to bed with you, Jan, I think I can trust you to keep your half of the bargain. And if I can't, at least it's worth a try."

She looked at him. She was not feeling in a sexy mood by any stretch of the imagination, and yet she could not look at this man who had once been her husband without feeling desire rush through every part of her body. Now he was there, ready to make love to her. It could be her last act in Coldwater, her one item of pleasure to take along when she left.

She took a deep breath.

Later, when she looked back on that particular moment in time, she realized that her action had been the most difficult she had ever performed. It wasn't anything that would have won her a medal, but it took some doing.

She did it.

"Forget it," she told him. "I'm getting out of town tonight anyway."

He stared at her as if he did not believe that he had heard her correctly.

"You heard right," she told him. "I figure I've milked this town for enough already. I'm getting out and I'm staying out for keeps."

"Where are you going?"

"Away. I'm not sure where."

He went on staring at her. There was a great need within her to leave him with some favorable impression of herself, to generate some spark of friendship or approval if not love within him. But she realized that the nicest thing she could do for him was to be as much of a bitch as possible. She had already strained his marriage as much as possible. So, whether it hurt her or not, she had to leave him with the impression that she was worthless scum. That would tighten the bond between him and his wife. It seemed a small enough wedding present.

"So there's no point in you making love to me," she said, her voice as tough and hard as she could make it. "For one thing, I've had enough men this past little while for a lifetime. And plenty of them were better in bed than you'll ever be."

She drew a breath. "Besides," she said, "you better save all the strength you've got for that little whore you married. It would take an army to handle her properly."

That did it, of course. He turned red, and he called her a few filthy names, and then he turned on his heel and stalked out of the trailer. The door slammed.

She ground out her cigarette. You hate me, she thought. Well, go ahead and hate me. Because that's the best thing for you right now. The more you manage to hate me, the better off you and your wife will be.

So hate me.

She knew that she would never see Jack Appleton again. And she knew that it was best that way, best for her and best for him, best all around. She thought about the men she would meet, and she thought about the man whom she would eventually marry.

And she wondered if she would ever learn to love that nameless and faceless man as much as she loved Jack Appleton. And she doubted it.

Then she did a very strange thing. She folded her arms on the desk top and lowered her face to meet them. And, for the first time in far too long, she cried.

"I CAN LIKE PICTURE it now," Royal Peters said. "Makes a pretty picture, it does. You want to hear about this picture I got in mind, girl?"

She knew the picture, knew it from beginning to end, knew every last detail of it.

"Tell me about it, Royal."

He warmed to his subject. "There's this little town," he said. "Little town over the line in Ohio. That's where the North really begins, you know. Where a colored man is a man, not a slave."

You're a slave all over, she thought. You've never been past Cinci in your life and I was born and bred in Harlem. But you tell me all about it, Royal lover. Tell me about The Dream. Make it good, baby.

"Just a little old little town," he went on. "Remember that movie we saw, girl?"

She nodded.

"What was the name of it?"

"*A Sound of Distant Drums.*"

"That's it," he said. "Remember the little town in that movie? The one Reed Schwerner was holed up in when the Indians came after him?"

She nodded.

"A town like that," he said positively. "And we'll have a little luncheonette in that town. Right on the main drag, a nice little luncheonette with that linoleum tile on the floor and a Formica-top counter and a handful of little tables. Makes a big difference when you get some good tiles on the floor. Hell, I know how to lay 'em."

You sure do, she thought.

"Just need to borrow a torch and slap 'em down," he said. "You can give me a hand with 'em. Have the whole floor done in a day or two at the outside. Keep that floor so clean you can eat off it. Then we open up for business."

Open for business, she thought. I ought to have a sign like that on my body.

"I can see it now," he went on. "I'll be back there with

my chef's hat on my head. Nice tall white hat, good and fancy. Let everybody think I know how to cook. Hell, I can learn fast enough. Any fool can cook once he gets a little practice."

You're cooking fine, she thought. You're cooking on all four burners, baby.

"And you in a red and white apron," he said. "All nice and starched and all. You'll be behind the counter, see. Or waiting on tables. Hell, I guess you'll have to handle the cashbox too, baby. You think I can trust you to take care of all the money we'll be making?"

That'll be the day, she thought. Here we are and *I'm* the one's making the money. And who's taking care of it?

"Now I got a surprise for you," he said. "Something sweet and pretty. Something to take all the edges off."

Pot, of course. Tea. The perennial answer.

"Something a little different, baby. Something that comes in powdered form. We can go a whole hell of a lot farther with this cooking in back of us, girl. A whole lot further."

She watched as he took a paper envelope from his pocket. He sprinkled a pile of white powder on a slim sheet of white paper. She knew what the powder was.

"I don't dig it," she told him.

"Ever make it?"

She shook her head. "That's hard stuff," she said. "You ride that little horse and you never get off. I know all about that stuff, Royal."

"Girl!" He was hurt now. "I ain't talking about any mainline action. You think I want you poking holes in your arms and legs? Not my woman."

Oh, no, she thought. Not in a million years.

"No needle games for us," he said. "That's for the junkies. We ain't about to become junkies, girl."

The hell we ain't, she thought.

"We just going to sniff a little," he told her. "Just a little sniffing action. Can't get hooked that way, girl. Nobody yet ever got hooked with a sniff."

Never, she thought. First you sniff. Then you joypop, you skin-pop, because it's a bigger kick that way and what the hell, the stuff costs you the same no matter what you do with it and you might as well get the biggest kick you can. And then you mainline for the same reason, and because the skin-pop isn't any fun any more, because you keep needing a little bit more of a kick, a little bit more of a boot.

And then you're hooked through the bag and back again, and it's thirty or forty bucks a day just to quiet the monkey. And then you look back and wonder where it was you got the hook in you. And you never shake it loose.

She had never tried heroin. She had turned it down time after time, sticking to pot because it wasn't habit forming and you could drop it whenever you wanted if you really wanted to. She had swung with pot and pot was always plenty, and she knew better than to go looking around for white ponies to ride.

"Come on, girl. Take a little sniff for Papa. One little sniff ain't going to hurt. You don't like it and we never make horse again. But how can you say you don't dig it if you never made it in the first place?"

The argument wasn't new. The arguments were never new—even when you heard them for the very first time they sounded old and worn.

This argument was ancient.

"Come on now, girl," he was saying. And he was holding the slip of paper with the heap of powder just an inch in front of her nose.

And she was an all-alone whore in a town she didn't like, a town that didn't like her at all. And he was all she had, all she would ever have, and the slip of paper was right there, and all the arguments against it kind of dropped away when you took all those things into consideration.

She sniffed up the powder.

For a few seconds nothing happened, and for a few seconds she thought that Royal had been sold a bill of goods, that the powder was nothing but chalk dust.

Then things began to happen.

And, all at once, she could see that luncheonette, that lunch counter that would exist forever in her dreams . . . and nowhere else. She saw it more clearly than she had ever seen it before.

It looked wonderful.

NIGHT.

The money was in a suitcase in the trunk of the car. The car was already across the state line. Kentucky was something to forget about forever, something that she had to tell herself over and over again had never happened.

She was on her way.

The trailer, the whorehouse on wheels, remained in its parking place at one end of the trailer camp. She could not have cared less what happened to it. They could sell it at auction, or they could fix it up as a museum and charge tourists admission to go look at it and bounce on the beds.

Or they could set it on fire and watch it burn, and let the kids toast marshmallows over the flames. Or they could roll it toward a hill—if they could find a hill—and pitch it over the top.

She did not care.

She cared only that she was done with it, that she would never see it again, just as she would never see the town or the people who lived in it. The town and the people were things she had to forget. The memories were bad memories, useless cargo to be jettisoned at the first opportunity.

She had a life ahead of her.

She wondered what kind of life it could be. She was still a young woman, by all rules, but at the same time she had already lived what would be termed a rather full life. She had been married and divorced. She had been a whore and a madam. And she had been a murderess a few times removed.

What was left?

That was a good question. It was one that she would answer in time. She had almost answered it already while driving the car out of Kentucky. There had been a turn in the road with a long drop over the hill if you didn't make the turn. She had been depressed, very depressed, and she very nearly didn't make the turn. It was easy—you just forced yourself to think about other things and before you knew it you were off the road and it was all over, all over forever.

But she had been unable to do it.

It had been too easy, too simple. And at the last minute her hands had given the wheel a wrench and she had stayed on the road, tires giving a small squeal of protest. You didn't kill yourself, not if you could help it. It was too damn easy, too simple. Life demanded more of you than that.

She wondered what would happen. Maybe in time she would kill herself. She hoped not.

But there was a time for that sort of thing, just as there was a time for everything else.

She wondered.

MY NEWSLETTER: I get out an email newsletter at unpredictable intervals, but rarely more often than every other week. I'll be happy to add you to the distribution list. A blank email to lawbloc@gmail.com with "newsletter" in the subject line will get you on the list, and a click of the "Unsubscribe" link will get you off it, should you ultimately decide you're happier without it.

LAWRENCE BLOCK is a Mystery Writers of America Grand Master. His work over the past half century has earned him multiple Edgar Allan Poe and Shamus awards, the U.K. Diamond Dagger for lifetime achievement, and recognition in Germany, France, Taiwan, and Japan. His latest novel is *Dead Girl Blues*; other recent fiction includes *A Time to Scatter Stones*, *Keller's Fedora*, and *The Burglar in Short Order*. In addition to novels and short fiction, he has written episodic television (*Tilt!*) and the Wong Kar-wai film, *My Blueberry Nights*.

Block contributed a fiction column in Writer's Digest for fourteen years, and has published several books for writers, including the classic *Telling Lies for Fun & Profit* and the updated and expanded *Writing the Novel from Plot to Print to Pixel*. His nonfiction has been collected in *The Crime of Our Lives* (about mystery fiction) and *Hunting Buffalo with Bent Nails* (about everything else). Most recently, his collection of columns about stamp collecting, *Generally Speaking*, has found a substantial audience throughout and far beyond the philatelic community.

Lawrence Block has lately found a new career as an anthologist (*At Home in the Dark*; *From Sea to Stormy Sea*) and holds the position of writer-in-residence at South Carolina's Newberry College. He is a modest and humble fellow, although you would never guess as much from this biographical note.

Email: lawbloc@gmail.com
Twitter: @LawrenceBlock
Facebook: lawrence.block
Website: lawrenceblock.com

9 798463 063359